URBAN JUSTICE

VIGILANTE JUSTICE THRILLER SERIES 3, WITH
JACK LAMBURT

JOHN ETZIL

For my Aunt Sophie, the last of the Greatest Generation.

You guys are awesome.

FREE BOOK

Join my VIP reader group and receive a FREE 20K word 'Thriller Shot' in the Jack Lamburt Vigilante Justice Series.

FAST Justice - Vigilante Justice Thriller Series 2.5 with Jack Lamburt

Details at the end of this book, along with a FREE preview of Fatal Justice & Airliner Down!

1

COSMO GRABBED Debbie by the ponytail and pushed the business end of the sawed-off shotgun against the underside of her chin. With a slight chuckle, he tilted her head backwards, forcing it until it couldn't go any further. A shiny gold-toothed grin spread across his face. His voice was soft, almost friendly, and I had no problem hearing what he said in the dead quiet of the Red Barn.

"It'd be a shame to spread this pretty lady's brains all over the ceiling, so which one of you is going to tell me what I need to know?"

Silence.

There were a handful of us inside the Red Barn that night. The bad guys had arrived a few minutes earlier, guns drawn, and forced us all to lie down on the floor. Except for the bartender, my girlfriend, Debbie.

"No takers? Let's make this a little more interesting,

then." He pried open Debbie's lips with the tip of the shotgun. "Come on, open up that pretty mouth of yours."

She did, and he slid the barrel in so deep that she coughed, her upper body flexing forward in response to the gag reflex.

"Better not do that again." He smirked and nodded to his shotgun. "She's cocked and ready to blow. I can't promise you that your gagging won't set her off."

Debbie regained her composure, her eyes never losing that focus that I'd come to love. She didn't sniffle, whimper, or tremble. No beads of sweat broke out on her forehead or upper lip. She glared into his eyes. Defiant until the end.

He kept the gun jammed in her mouth and turned her around so that her back was to us. He raised the handle of the shotgun, pointing it downwards towards us and forcing her to lean over backwards.

"Now. I'll ask you folks one more time before I splatter her brains all over you. Who hired you to take Catherine?"

Nobody inside the Red Barn knew Catherine, or anything else about Cosmo and why he'd paid us a visit. Except for Debbie and me. The others all looked at each other, the expressions on their ashen faces switching from fear, to confusion, and then back again.

Rodney was the first to speak up, the two-beer superman effect having lifted him from the floor and into a standing position.

"She don't know nothing. Now you leave us be. Take your kind and get out of here."

"My kind?" Cosmo's voice crackled, his eyes widened, and I could tell that he was about ready to blow a fuse. "My freakin' kind?" He removed the shotgun from Debbie's mouth and leveled it at Rodney.

Uh-oh...

2

A FEW WEEKS EARLIER, I had been sitting at the bar in the Red Barn in Summit, New York, where Debbie was fielding compliments from her liquored-up admirers. Located about an hour's drive west of Albany, Summit had a population that hovered around a thousand, and the Red Barn, being the only entertainment in town, did a nice little business.

It was a simple place, a single restroom in the side wall next to the kitchen, an old jukebox that actually spun 45 records, and a sawdust-covered dance floor for when the customers drank enough beer to kill their inhibitions.

As soon as I walked in, my number one fan signaled me from the far end of the bar and waved me over. Frances was at it again. Perched on her stool, straight as an arrow, the ninety-four-year-old white-haired lady that was the spitting image of Granny Clampett raised her glass of whiskey and smiled at me. "Sheriff Joe, come drink with me. I'm buying."

She sucked on her cigarette and blew the smoke out through her toothless grin.

My name's really Jack, and I'd replaced Sheriff Joe after he retired a few years ago, but Frances didn't seem to remember.

"Sure, just give me a minute and I'll be right over." She'd been hounding me to drink with her since the first day I'd walked into this place, and I hoped that after a few minutes, she'd forget my latest acceptance to her offer and not have her feelings hurt when I didn't cozy up next to her.

I sat down on my usual stool at the bar, where I could watch the door, and my Debbie, as she worked the barstool crowd and fattened her tip jar. God, she was good at what she did.

I'd met Debbie my first night back in town, and like every other schmo at the Red Barn, her beauty had captured my heart the moment I'd seen her. It wasn't just her long legs, big breasts, Hollywood smile, and almond-shaped eyes that lit up when she saw me. It was the way she carried herself. Hidden under all that flirty tip-gathering banter, was a commanding presence that was impossible for me to miss. Some guys never saw it, others might be intimidated by it. But not me. I relished it.

She came over to me, placed a Molson XXX on the bar, and smirked at me. "You know, Frances's been asking you to have a drink with her for a while now. It'd be nice if you made her night."

"She's just so touchy-feely." I took a sip of ice-cold beer

and smiled. "She's lucky I don't arrest her for sexual assault. The list of guys she's ass-grabbed is pretty expansive."

"Oh, stop, she's harmless. Just deal with it. You know she's crazy about you."

"Fine. But I'm taking you home tonight."

"Oh? I don't know about that." She head-waved over towards Bobby, a local drunk with a super big crush on Debbie. He was sitting in his usual place at the middle of the bar. Getting drunk. "Bobby did his good deed for the night. He went over and chatted with Frances for a good half hour."

"At your suggestion, no doubt."

"True. But just the same, him taking the time to do that has him looking pretty fine to me tonight." She smiled her appreciation over to Bobby, who replied with a wink and a smile of his own.

"Okay, fine." I grabbed my beer and headed over to Frances.

Out of the corner of my eye, I saw Debbie go over to the middle of the bar and wash some whiskey glasses in the sink in front of Bobby. I looked in the mirror behind the bar and watched his eyes triple in size when he caught sight of her cleavage. He smiled so hard that I thought his face was going to crack. Now I knew why he always sat on that same stool every night.

Frances spotted me walking over to her and smiled at me. She slid the stool next to her away from the bar and patted it. "Sit Sheriff Joe. Take a load off."

"Hey, Frances. How you doing?" I sat down and placed my beer on the bar.

"Fine, Sheriff. How about you?"

I looked over at Debbie and frowned. She was really giving Bobby an eyeful as she leaned over into the cooler and retrieved a frosted mug for another one of her loyal fans. "Oh, just fine."

"She really likes you, ya know."

"Huh?" I turned to Frances. "You mean Debbie?"

"No, I mean Aunt Jemima. Of course I mean Debbie. I can tell by the way she looks at you." She reached across the bar and picked up her pack of Lucky Strikes, shook one out, and put it between her lips. "Ahem. A real gentleman would light his lady's smoke."

I looked down at the white pack of cigarettes with the big red circle. "I thought you gave up the Luckies?"

"Nah. I tried those Marlboro Reds. They just didn't do it for me. Not strong enough."

I grabbed her silver lighter from the bar and flicked it open. I was in full disclaimer mode. "Okay, but this goes against my better judgment."

She laughed. "What're you, a lawyer now?"

"No, ma'am, please don't ever accuse me of that." I chuckled and drank some beer. She laughed and blew smoke out in the other direction.

"I've been a people watcher for a long time. I can tell she really likes you."

"That's good to know."

"Stop playing so nonchalant. I can also tell you *really* like her."

"Yes, I like her." I took a sip of beer and changed the subject. "So what's new with you?"

"New with me? Jack, dear—and yes, I remember your real name—I'm almost ninety-five. Nothing's new at this age. So stop trying to change the subject." She took a drag on her smoke and pointed to Debbie. "She reminds me of someone else that used to look at you like that. Remember? In high school?"

Oh, jeez. Here we go. Nothing's worse than an old fogey reminiscing about something from twenty years ago. I knew I shouldn't have sat next to her, but I had to be pleasant. "What do you mean?"

"When you were a junior, or senior, at Richmondville High School. I can't remember which. It was my last year there before I was forced to retire. You and I didn't have a lot of interaction, me being a librarian and you being a jock and all. But I do remember a certain someone who used to look at you the same exact way that Debbie does. I can't remember her name, but I'll think of it..."

"Ah, yeah, high school. The good old days." I drank some beer and looked at Debbie. She winked at me and smiled. I couldn't wait to get her home. I started daydreaming about how I was going to pour her some red wine, light a small fire for atmosphere, put on some Barry White, and—

"Meredith!" Francis banged her hand on the bar and

jolted me out of my fantasy. "That's her name. She's Mary Sue's mom, married to that doctor guy. I see them around here once in a while."

Meredith? What the? Where was this going? I did my best to sound disinterested. "Oh yeah. She's married to Stuart. He's a heart doctor. Is he your doctor?"

"*My* doctor? Heck no, Jack. I don't need no stinking doctor. They'll just kill you." She took a deep drag on her cigarette and flicked an ash on the floor. "Anyway, I see the way you look at Mary Sue too."

"Mary Sue? The waitress?" I scoffed at her. "Why, Frances! She's young enough to be my daughter."

"I know, that's what I mean. She has your eyes."

I looked at her and saw she was staring at me. No smile, no smirk, just a study in observation. I broke eye contact and stood up. "Well, nice chatting with you, Frances, but I've got to go play some pool with Max and Gus." I pointed over to the pool table, where the two older men were battling away against each other.

"Hold on, Jack." She placed a hand on my elbow. "Sit back down. I need to thank you properly."

"Huh? What for?" I sat back in my stool and took a swallow.

"Remember when these two city hoodlums were here? And that one cracked me across the shoulder and made me spill my whiskey? Well, I never got the chance to thank you for taking care of business."

I wasn't sure if she winked at me or had smoke in her

eye. "Oh, that's okay. Just doing my job, ma'am." I gripped the rim of my hat and gave it a tug, trying to look and sound like Marshal Dillon from *Gunsmoke*. "Now if you'll excuse me, ma'am, I don't want to keep my fellow pool players waiting."

"Oh, don't worry about Max and Gus. They ain't going anywhere. Besides, I'll make it up to them tonight after we get home."

What the? Dear God, did she just say what I thought she said?

"Anyhow, I know that you did more than your job. When Mary Sue and Debbie were steering me away from the commotion, I noticed you sitting by the end of the bar, smiling. I thought that odd at the time. Anyway, while the ruckus was going on, I snuck over and found the shotgun that Debbie keeps nice and shiny behind the bar. I hoped I didn't have to use it. That twelve-gauge makes such a mess, and it leaves a nasty bruise on my shoulder." She grabbed at her right shoulder and raised her elbow in a circular motion, working out the imaginary soreness. "As luck would have it, our fine Summit men took care of the two scoundrels. I looked over to you, and you'd gotten up and left. Now I know you're not running from any fight. So I think to myself, what's our fine sheriff up to now? So I went over to the small window behind the bar. I stood on my toes and watched you let yourself into the backseat of their SUV. You stayed there until they drove away, and they were never to be heard from again."

She took a sip of whiskey and a drag on her cigarette and continued, "A few days after that, I read an article in the paper about some missing mobsters. Turns out that our friends were the ones who went missing."

"Yeah, I read that too. Seems that they joined the witness protection program. By this time, they're probably at their new home in Arizona. Good riddance to them." I raised my beer mug and we clinked glasses.

"You know as well as I do that they didn't join anything, except the worm food club."

I looked over at her again. She was staring at me like before, except this time, she was smiling. "Don't worry, Jack, your secrets are safe with me." She nodded, downed her whiskey, and winked at me. "All of them."

3

I PLAYED a few games of pool with Max and Gus, but I was just going through the motions. I couldn't let go of what Frances had said. How had she figured all that out? Meredith? Mary Sue? Was it that easy? If *she* could see right through me, then I had big problems.

I finished up my last game and went back to the bar. I took my normal stool and Debbie came over to me with a fresh beer. "I need your help with something."

"Sure, babe, what's up?"

"I'm worried about my sister. I called all my friends, her friends, our relatives, and nobody has heard from Catherine in months."

"After the Sparky's Massacre, I was afraid of that. Those guys she was hanging with are bad. Where was she last heard from?"

"I don't know. Can you use TOR and HFS to look for her?"

TOR is an anonymous web browser that protects the user's privacy. HFS, or Home Front Security, is a little-known domestic super spy agency that I'd helped start when I worked at NSA. After a couple of years I'd burned out from the spying. That's what I told everyone, anyway. The real reason I'd left was frustration. HFS's mandate was to capture terrorists in this country before they could act. So, we spied on everybody. We uncovered a tremendous amount of bad people doing awful things. We found big-time drug dealers, mobsters, child sex traffickers, assassins, corrupt politicians, secretive white supremacist groups. A never-ending list of horrible people. But if it wasn't terror-related, HFS wasn't interested, so we just passed the info on to the FBI and forgot about it. The FBI had their hands tied. They couldn't make arrests on illegally gained intel because the courts would throw them out. Their only option was to start an investigation and get their own intel. Legally. But they didn't have enough manpower to open a case for each file we gave them, so maybe one in fifty was acted on.

I was working my way through the rest.

Flight 2262 had ignited a firestorm in me, and the only way that I could quench it was to stay involved in HFS. So I kept my hand in the game by working as an outside contractor for them. My area of expertise was IT—specifically, archiving, securing, and retrieving humongous amounts of data—and my top-secret security clearance allowed me to eavesdrop on anyone who had a pulse. If anyone could locate Catherine, it was me.

"Sure, I'll get started tomorrow," I said. "You have a cell number for her? Last known address and list of friends? Her birthdate and Social Security number would help too."

"Yeah, I'll email all that over to you," She looked at me and smiled. "Thanks so much, Jack. You don't know how much this means to me." She reached across the bar and hugged me. Her long black hair smelled like heaven, and I squeezed her tight and nibbled on her neck.

Out of the corner of my eye, I caught envious looks from every male sitting at the bar. Especially Bobby. I made eye contact with him and gave him a thumbs-up and a big smile.

Further down the bar, Frances was giving me imaginary high fives, complete with the ashes from her Lucky Strike falling into her hair. I smiled at her, all the while praying that she wouldn't set herself on fire. I turned my attention back to Debbie.

"So does that mean that you'll come home with me tonight instead of Bobbie?"

She broke our hug and chuckled. "Not sure yet. Let's see how the night plays out." She smiled and stuck her tongue out at me.

I normally loved her sense of humor, but enough was enough. I decided to play hardball. I nodded toward Bobby. "You know, guys who drink a lot have a—ahem, rigidity problem." I stood up and stuck my chest out, posing like a modern-day Tarzan. "Certainly not the case with me."

"Oh, don't worry about Bobby," she shot back with a wink. "That's what Viagra is for."

She walked over and got Bobby a fresh beer mug from the cooler, bending over right in front of him. He wiped the drool from his open mouth. He looked at me *after* she straightened up, and gave me a thumbs-up and a smile.

4

DESPITE MY HONEY'S propensity for torturing me with her wannabe suitors at the Red Barn, she did come home with me, and it was everything I'd dreamt about. Alas, morning eventually came, and she departed after breakfast, leaving me to spool up my TOR browser and log in to Home Front Security to research her sister's whereabouts.

My top-secret vendor credentials give me unrestricted access to all of HFS's data. If the average American knew how extensive the government's eavesdropping technology was, they'd shit their pants. HFS had unrestricted access *and* control of every single electronic device known to man.

All manufacturers that wanted to sell their electronic products in the land of the free, had to install a government-designed chip, through which HFS could admin the entire device. So if your device was, say, a TV, we could watch and record *you*. Same with a computer or a smartphone. Want to know how I was so sure about drunken Bobby's, ahem, rigidity problem? Never mind...

For devices with built-in motion detectors, like your common wall switch or outdoor lighting fixtures, our government techies took it a few dozen steps further and designed a sensor that had IR facial recognition. Show me a photo of a person's face, and I'd get you their latest location, along with their history at that location.

Those pesky red light cameras that snap a photo of you when you don't come to a full stop before making that right turn on red? All front seat occupants of *every* car got a facial IR scan.

If that wasn't enough to create paranoia, every electronic device in your life has audio recording capability. Want to know the real reason why the United States government wanted a smoke detector in every room? Yeah, exactly. And with our advanced voice recognition software, we only needed a voice sample of three seconds to positively identify a person with 99.9 percent accuracy.

Even if you didn't bother to set up your Wi-Fi–connected device when it was installed, we did you a solid and took care of it for you. You're welcome.

Don't have internet service? No problem. We created free Wi-Fi, under the pretense of "free internet for everyone," for just that reason. You, and every electronic device in your world, are online.

With all that tech on my side, I figured I'd locate Catherine right way. I even had a mental to-do list of things to take care of around the house after I gathered enough info on her to put together a kidnapping/rescue plan with the added bonus of killing a few bad guys, which, by the way, is my reason for living. The horrific events of Flight 2262 had turned me into a stone-cold vigilante, and I had a thirst for revenge that could only be quenched by bad guys dying, preferably in groups of ten.

After a few hours of ham-fingered inputs in the search box in the HFS database, I came up with enough information on Catherine to call it a day. It was a bittersweet accomplishment. Each time I clicked open a new window, I was hit with more and more depressing information about her. Poor kid was in deep. Drugs, stripping, gang affiliation, and prostitution. Damn.

I couldn't give my findings to Debbie over the phone. I needed to break it to her in person. I printed out a security camera photo for Debbie to positively identify the gaunt and disshelved person as Catherine, and shoved it in my pocket.

I let my Doberman pinscher Saber out to frolic in the backyard for a while. The rabbits that London, my hero German shepherd, used to chase around the yard were still living under the shed, but Saber didn't have the same herding instinct that London had possessed. Other than staring them down, which he did to everything that had eyes, he left them alone.

I opened the back door and he was sitting statuesque, his back to the house as he surveyed his domain, before turning and coming inside. I filled his water bowl and hopped into my truck while he watched me from the living room window.

I drove slow and took the long way to the Red Barn, taking the extra time to go over in my mind the conversation that I didn't look forward to having with Debbie. I arrived right before they opened and caught Debbie just as she'd finished setting up. She greeted me with her usual good humor. "I'm sorry, sir, we're closed. Come back later."

I hugged her and took her by the hand into the parking lot.

"Okay," she exhaled. "This can't be good. You're either breaking up with me, or you have some really bad news about Catherine. So, is this the luckiest day of Bobby's life, or not?"

"Not." I handed her the photo. Her expression told me that I'd found the right person, and that she was as equally disturbed at seeing it as I was.

I put my arm around her shoulder. "I'm sorry, babe, she's not doing well. She's a stripper, a heroin addict, and affiliated with a gang." I left out the prostitution part.

"Gangs? Heroin?" She looked up at me. "Are you kidding me?"

"No, I wish I was. Right now she's keeping company with a low-level drug dealer in Newburgh, named Roberto. It took me awhile to find her since they're kind of in the stone age as far as electronics go. Did you know that only six point four percent of Newburgh residents have microwaves? And that there are zero thermostats that contain Wi-Fi capabilities in the entire city."

"Uhhm, Patrick?" She rolled her eyes at me and shook her head.

Now I'd done it. Whenever she referred to me as that dumb-as-a-rock *SpongeBob* character, I knew I'd messed up big-time.

"I'm being nice to you because you're helping me out here, but who gives a shit about how many microwaves there are in Newburgh?"

"Well, I was just mentioning it because household electronic devices are how HFS gathers its intel, and a lack of said devices makes it harder to—"

"Patrick!" She pushed me away and stop-signed an open palm inches from my nose. "Shut up. Nobody freakin' cares!"

"Right. Well. Anyhow, at least we can go get her now."

"You have a plan?"

I stuck my chest out. "As a matter of fact, I do."

"Good. After tonight, I'm off for two days. Can we get her tomorrow?"

"Yes. I'll spend the rest of the day planning the mission." I gave her a hug. "Really sorry about this, babe. But we'll get her. I promise."

"I know we will." She wiped a tear from her face. "I know we will. See you tonight." She turned and went inside the Red Barn.

I climbed into my truck and headed back to Eminence. I

had a lot of packing to do, and despite my absolute confidence in my killing skill, this type of mission was a little outside my area of expertise. Kill everyone on site? Sure, no problem. Leave the scene with a live person? Never done that in my life.

5

I SPENT the rest of the day planning. I learned a lot about Newburgh and the drug trade as well as gangs that had taken over the city. The gang that Catherine was hanging with, the Silent But Deadly Aces, was especially violent. SBDA was headquartered in Camden, New Jersey, and had a satellite branch that dominated the Newburgh drug trade. The gang's MO was simple: befriend strippers, ply them with cheap heroin, and turn them into prostitutes who'd work for their fix.

After a short stint as a prostitute, Catherine had managed to work herself into the upper echelon of the group. She didn't have to walk the streets anymore, but she still had to service gang members as a favor to the boss. She was basically a gang slave, and in return she was protected, well fed, and supplied with heroin, keeping her addicted for as long as she looked hot and did what was asked of her.

Previous girlfriends who had failed at either of those two tasks had gone missing—either traded away to another gang like an old baseball card, or dumped in the Hudson River.

My kill list from HFS research had grown to over a hundred, but I had no SBDA members on it. Until now. I promoted Roberto to numero uno and grinned as I rubbed my palms together in excitement. As many times as I killed a bad guy, the thrill of an upcoming mission of evildoer destruction never got old.

Through HFS research I found a shady real estate broker in Newburgh, Jimmy the Guinea—swear to God that was his name—who specialized in rental units. My request was a little unique, and I could tell from his initial "you want a what?" that he was taken aback.

I requested a unit that was in an abandoned building so I didn't have to worry about any interaction with the neighbors. We should be mission complete in a day or two, but I had to plan for a longer stay just in case my intel was off. Or if something went wrong. I'd been on enough of these types of missions to realize that things usually didn't go as planned. And as a six-foot-six lily-white person of zero color in the mostly minority demographic of Newburgh, I was going to stand out like a fat-fingered proctologist who gave lectures on how to ease a patient's anxiety about their upcoming prostate exam.

Using a fictitious identity and a burner phone, I bitcoined Jimmy the Guinea the hefty sum of two thousand dollars for a one-month rental on Landers Street, the heart of Newburgh's gangland territory. He commented about how I must really love the area to be willing to pay so much. I told him that my offer included a little extra for him to keep a secret, and that I expected him to comply. He joked that for that much coin, I could have his wife for the duration of my stay as well.

Although I appreciated his generosity, I told him to shut the hell up. It didn't help that in my HFS research, I'd stumbled across a photo of his wife stepping out of the shower, and let's just say she left a lot to be desired in the body-grooming category. Hairy armpits and upper lips aren't my thing.

I went out to my garage, removed the license plate from my truck, and put on a burner plate that I'd bought online from a company in China. I'd had it shipped to one of my secret PO boxes. Burner plates were a lot more complex than burner phones. I had to hack into the New York Department of Motor Vehicles website and search for the same model, year, and color Toyota that I had. Once I found that, I had to make sure that there were no outstanding warrants or unpaid tickets on the plates. This way, if a law enforcement officer called in my plates, they'd come back clean. If he or she happened to pull me over, then they'd either buy my story that my friend had lent me his truck, or I'd be forced to go down a path I really didn't want to go, but would if needed.

Now that the hospitality and travel logistics were taken

care of, I focused on weaponry. I knew that my trusty Glock 17 with Osprey silencer would, as always, be my main pistol. I loaded up my go bag with some duct tape, cable ties, a spool of paracord, night vision binoculars, a police scanner, sodium pentothal, ecstasy tabs, a pair of heavy-duty wire cutters, and three spare Glock 17s, which you can never have too many of. I wasn't a fan of those clowns who owned ten different handguns in their quest to impress others. In their quest to cover up their small junk insecurities, they could spout out gun manufacturer acronyms like they were reciting their ABCs in grammar school. "Yeah, I've got an H&K, S&W, Sig Sau, yada yada yada..." It was all bullshit. I *did* have ten handguns, but they were all Glock 17s. And all of them had at least one notch in them.

I threw in a dozen or so extra ammo magazines, like most people toss spare change into a jar, and topped it all off with my Kindle.

I popped open my drone case and made sure that both batteries were fully charged, then closed it back up. That was another benefit of being an HFS vendor. They had the neatest James Bond–type gizmos that I could "test." And this drone—I'd named her Amelia—topped the list. She was a quadcopter the size of an iPad, and stealthy enough that she couldn't be heard if she was flying over two hundred feet high, so it was perfect for surveillance.

The best part about Amelia was the mapping software that came with her. Using my iPhone, I could program her to take off, fly to any height and in any direction as fast or slow as I wanted, and collect 4K video as well as gigantic 48MP still images. She had the equivalent of a 400mm tele-photo lens on her stealthy frame, allowing me to zoom in and read the circulation date of a dime from two hundred feet.

Once the route was planned out, I pressed the GO button, and Amelia took care of the rest. Priceless.

I debated taking my newly acquired Remington 700 bolt action .308 rifle with suppressor, night vision scope, and laser. I'd picked one up after the Sparky's Tavern Massacre, and although I had no plans of sniping anyone, I thought it would be a great tool for Debbie to back me up with, so I decided to take it with us.

My second go bag had a couple of burner phones in a lead-shielded bag to make them untraceable, along with a healthy amount of bottled water, protein bars, and other snacks. Since eating Newburgh food wasn't an option, that would have to tide us over until mission completion. I threw in one change of clothes just in case I got smeared with Roberto's DNA and had to burn the ones I had on. A worthy sacrifice to kill that little bastard.

Little did I know that for the first time in my post Flight 2262 life, I'd fail on a mission.

FBI AGENT LEO KENNEDY knocked on his supervisor's open door and waited for him to look up from his paperwork before entering his office.

"Can I have a moment with you, sir?"

"Sure, Leo, what's up?"

"It's the Agent Skillman case, and that Sheriff Lamburt fellow."

Paul Cefalo, Special Agent in charge of the Newburgh office, put his pen down and gave Leo his undivided attention. "Go on."

"I still can't shake that feeling, sir. Something's just not right with that guy."

"You sure it's not because he pointed a gun at you and nearly made you piss your pants?"

"No, that's not it. I mean, that's messed up and all, but there's more. When we interviewed the patrons of the Red

Barn to find out if anyone had seen Agent Skillman before he disappeared, that one old lady's comments really stuck in my mind."

"You mean the old lady that grabbed your ass and told you to go screw yourself?"

"Yes, but before that she talked about Sheriff Lamburt taking care of their own. Kind of like in a threatening manner."

"I read that in your report, Leo. Now, is there anything else?"

"I'd like permission to look into this guy's background a little deeper. Maybe even go up to Summit and snoop around a little. I still think there might be something there."

Paul frowned, stood up, and walked over and closed his door. He gestured to a chair. "Sit down, Leo."

He sat back down at his desk. "I don't know if you know this or not, but Sheriff Lamburt is a Flight 2262 survivor. Unfortunately, his wife wasn't so lucky. He also had a stellar career with the CIA before moving over to the NSA, where he worked on top-secret assignments. I really don't think that there's anything there, but if you want to take a cursory look, then go ahead. Just make it quick. We've got a backlog of cases, and with Congress just cutting our budget, this office is short a man, so I can't afford to have you spending too much time on a wild goose chase."

"Understood, sir." Agent Kennedy stood up. "Anything else?"

"Yes. Lamburt's father is a big political donor. Both

parties. He has many friends in high places. Make sure you have something rock-solid on him before you ruffle any feathers. Understood?"

"Yes, sir. Understood. Thank you, sir."

"Good. That's all. Leave the door open."

Agent Kennedy turned and left the office, all the while planning out the next steps of his investigation of Sheriff Jack Lamburt.

CATHERINE SNUGGLED up to Roberto on his couch and slid her hand down his pants, landing on his crotch. She whispered in his ear, "Hey, baby, how about a little TLC?"

"Not now. But I do need you to do me a favor." He took out a burner cell phone and dialed. The call was answered on the second ring.

"Yeah."

"Yo, Jorge, what's up, dude?"

"Hey, man. I'm busy. This important?"

"Yeah, bro, your favorite girl's here. She's ready for some action." Roberto looked at Catherine, winked, and stroked her bare thigh.

"No shit? Catherine? I'll be right over."

"Cool, dude. See you in a few." He hung up the flip phone and removed its battery so that it couldn't be traced. Too bad he didn't know that the newer flip phones had a small rechargeable internal battery that couldn't be disconnected, and that HFS was recording all of his calls and texts, and tracking his movements. HFS was also logged in to his microwave and fridge, as well as his electric razor.

Catherine kissed Roberto on the neck. "Baby, I'm not really in the mood for Jorge. Can't it just be me and you?"

Roberto's face reddened, and he pushed her away so hard that she fell off the couch and onto the floor. He stood over her and grabbed a handful of hair. "Not in the mood? Now you listen to me, you stupid bitch. Cosmo told you to obey me. Jorge's my friend. You take care of him. Or else I'll tell Cosmo that his whore didn't treat me right. And we know what happens to Cosmos's whores when they step out of line, right?" He raised an open hand over his head, the threat clear. "Understand?"

She nodded yes.

He released her hair and pushed her backwards until she lay on her back on the floor. Her knees were up in the air, and her miniskirt covered nothing. He didn't allow her to wear any panties, and he got a full view of her freshly shaved pussy. His brain short-circuited, and any logical thought, however minute, came to a screeching halt. He reverted back to his Neanderthal brain and lost control.

"Holy shit, that's hot." He knelt down between her legs and pulled her T-shirt up, bra and all, and covered her face with it. "Jesus God, your tits are so fucking big."

He undid his jeans and slid into her. "Oh. Fuck. So. Good." He held her arms outstretched over her head and groaned into her neck. She crossed her ankles behind his back and pulled him in tight. He pumped her hard, and after a few seconds he let out a moan and collapsed on top of her.

"Wow, that was fuckin' great." He knelt up between her legs and zipped up his jeans. She pulled her shirt down, smearing her mascara, and she went to kiss him. He pushed her away. "Goddammit, Catherine, go put your fuckin' face on. I can't let Jorge see you like that. Dumb bitch."

She got up and went into the bathroom. She tousled her hair in front of the cracked mirror and fixed her makeup. She removed her shirt and bra and hung the bra over a towel rack. She put her shirt back on, turned sideways, and smiled at the way her tight shirt accentuated her busty profile.

She felt some of Roberto leaking down her leg, so she grabbed a tissue and wiped him off, wondering if Jorge knew that he'd be getting sloppy seconds. Or, if he even cared.

When she came out, Roberto and Jorge were sitting on the couch with a small line of heroin on a mirror on the coffee table in front of them. She dropped to her knees and helped herself to the one thing in her life that buried the pain of the past. The death of her sister Tiffany, of her parents, and worst of all, of her hopes and dreams.

When she finished, she smiled up at the two men, removed her shirt, and shoulder-waved her breasts at them with a giggle.

"Holy shit." Jorge's eyes stuck to her tits like bugs on flypaper. "Wow. Fuckin' wow. No matter how many times I see those things..." He adjusted his crotch and squirmed in his seat.

Roberto smiled, stood up, and helped her up by the arm. "Let's go to the bedroom."

8

I WENT over the plan of action two more times, start to finish, before pouring a glass of Makers Mark and popping a bottle of Debbie's favorite red wine. I spooled up Barry White on iTunes and put a single log in the fireplace. A moderate spring night in upstate NY didn't really warrant a fire, but you couldn't beat one for romantic atmosphere.

I let Saber out for the final time of the night before stripping down and hitting the shower. The night before I left on a mission always made me feel extra alive, and with Debbie coming over after she finished work, I knew that it was going to be a long and delicious night.

I was right.

We spent the following day going over and fine-tuning our plans, trying to think of all kinds of ways that it could change mid-mission, and how we'd have to adjust on the fly. Everything from surveillance cameras to police cruisers to well-armed gang members was discussed. She loved the idea of the Remington 700, so I patted myself on the back for picking one up recently.

We took a short nap in the afternoon to acclimate our sleep schedule to the late nights that were to follow. Places like Newburgh didn't come alive until after dark. Just about the same time that I normally hit the sack. I was an early riser, usually by five a.m., so this was going to be a big change for me. Not so much for Debbie, who was used to working late at the Red Barn.

We showered, separately so I wouldn't be distracted, and settled down at the kitchen table for the last good meal we'd have for a while.

After dinner, I tossed our bags into the extended cab of my Toyota, which turned out to be the perfect vehicle for this mission. Dark-colored and old, it would fit well into the tired and run-down Newburgh landscape.

We left shortly after that, leaving our cell phones and E-ZPass on the kitchen counter. I often had Mary Sue house- and pet-sit when I went on missions, but this one was so close to home and should only be a few days, so I decided to take Saber with us. If things worked out well, we'd be back before anyone realized that we were gone.

Our plan was to make the trip at a leisurely pace and arrive a little before dark. With my lily-white skin and her beautiful looks, we were sure to draw attention to ourselves, so we didn't want to spend too much time in daylight. As an added precaution, I had Debbie wear a baseball hat, big sunglasses, and baggy old clothes to minimize her stunning figure.

The trip to Newburgh was one hundred and eight miles, which took us two hours before we were rolling down Landers Street, also known as Blood Alley, for the violence that took place there.

Wow, what a change from Eminence.

The majority of the houses were decrepit two- and three-story structures, either row homes or jammed so close together that you could barely walk between them. Most of the homes were brick-faced, but the trim and porch areas were rotten wood that, except for graffiti gang markings, hadn't seen a coat of paint since the eighties. Many of the homes had boarded-up windows, and some even had their street addresses spray-painted across the front of them.

Front yards were nonexistent, and the street was littered with garbage and ratty old tied-up sneakers hanging from the overhead wires. Decrepit and abandoned cars lined the broken-up curbs, and the road was filled with potholes and rusty old storm drain covers.

"Holy shit," Debbie said.

"I know, right? People in America actually live like this... what a shame."

"You think your truck will be safe here?"

"I don't know, but we can't worry about that. Let's just find our building."

We drove around the neighborhood to get a feel for it, drawing our fair share of staredowns from the street toughs.

Too bad I was here for Catherine and couldn't afford to be distracted, or I could have had some real fun with these clowns. I made a mental note to plan a return trip after the smoke cleared from this one. I had a hunch that might take some time, though. Rescue mission or not, I was determined to leave a trail of dead evildoers.

We found a parking lot behind a closed-down industrial complex and I pulled my Toyota in. I pressed the button on Amelia's app and brought up the route I had created earlier for her to fly. I had to modify it some, since her launch location was off by a few blocks, but in no time she was prepped and ready to go.

I launched Amelia and watched her fly away. Her mission was to collect video and still photos of the heroin house, and I had no doubt that she'd succeed.

I watched the live feed on my iPhone, impressed with her flying precision and the quality of the 4K video and telephoto lens. Fifteen minutes and five orbits around the heroin house later, my intrepid aviatrix ended her mission and headed for the bed of my pickup, where she made a perfect landing.

We drove around some more, and by the time we pulled up in front of our rental unit, the sun had set and night was fast approaching. Our living quarters for the next few days was a middle-of-the-block three-story red brick-face that was covered in dead ivy and graffiti. Some of the windows on the first floor were boarded up, but the second- and third-floor windows were intact. There were a few other cars parked on the street, all old, and most with parking tickets shoved under their beaten-up wiper blades. As if these poor folks had the cash to pay them...

A walkway on both sides of the building led to a tiny fenced-in rear yard. Debris and runaway weed growth covered most of it. We led Saber, off leash, into the backyard, where he took care of business. I found the third slate stepping stone from the rear door. I picked it up and found the envelope that contained the key to our unit. We got our luggage and keyed our way up to the second floor, which had a small landing at the top of the stairs. Our unit, 2C, was one of three doors. I unlocked the door and stepped inside.

Holy crap.

Now I know what Jimmy the Guinea had meant when he'd said I must really like this place to pay so much money for it. The ceilings had big pieces of paint peeling from them, so much that it looked like a vermiculite in a cave. The light-colored walls were stained by cigarette smoke, and I could easily identify where posters used to hang. And this was before I turned the lights on.

The flooring was painted plywood. Piles of garbage were swept into the corners, and the minimal amount of furniture was all broken, which was fine with me because we weren't going to use it anyway.

I switched on the lights in the kitchen and stuff scurried. Mostly cockroaches, with a couple of mice and a rat or two thrown in for good measure.

All that was child's play compared to the stench that greeted us. Debbie fought back a gag and commented that she'd rather kiss an elephant's ass after a two-week bout of dysentery than stay in this place.

"All for your sister, dear, all for your sister."

I put my arm around her shoulder and posed us in the doorway, like a happy couple moving into their first home together. I raised my burner phone with a chuckle. "Let's take a selfie."

She laughed and elbowed me in the gut.

I closed the door, and we set our go bags down in the center of the living room, then checked out the other rooms in our unit. As expected, it was more of the same.

We heard people racing up the stairwell, their curses echoing through the building. I reached for my Glock and followed Saber over to the door. When the group reached the landing of our floor, they started banging on the door to the apartment next to us. "Open up, you bitch!"

I shook my head and looked at Debbie. "Isn't this just perfect?"

"Where's my gun?" she whispered.

I went over to my go bag and pulled out a holstered Glock. I handed it to her and started to explain the intricacies of the fine work of art. She stared at me with a deadpan face.

"Really, Jack?" She held the Glock out in front of her. "I've got over five hundred kills in my military career, and you're going to explain to *me* how this works?"

"Well, I mean, there's no denying you're proficient with a sniper rifle, but—"

"Patrick. Stop talking. Right now, or I'll order Saber to bite you in the nuts."

I nodded my understanding.

She sighed and shook her head. She closed her eyes, popped out the magazine, cleared the chamber, dry-fired in a safe direction, pulled the slide pins down, slid the rail off, popped the spring off, and removed the barrel. A complete breakdown.

"Time?" she asked, her eyes still closed.

"Uhm. I wasn't timing you, but maybe four seconds?"

A few seconds later she had it all back together with a round in the chamber. She put it back in the holster, and opened her eyes.

Holy shit. That was impressive.

The door banging and shouting continued, and I nodded towards it, "So what now?"

Debbie shook her head. "No. We can't get involved. We have a mission to accomplish, and this will set us back."

I frowned, hating the disappointment of missing a confrontation with a couple of douche bags. "Yeah, I guess you're right. I hate to waste the opportunity, though..."

"Just let it go."

I holstered my Glock and grabbed our bags. "Let's do an equipment check." I hoped the distraction of our work would deaden the noise from next door, which had morphed from loud banging and cursing into a woman crying and cursing. Jeez, this place had a lot of drama. So much for the abandoned building Jimmy the Guinea promised me.

We sat down on the floor and unpacked one of the go bags, spreading the weapons out in a circle around us, which gave me a warm fuzzy. I pocketed the police scanner and took the Remington 700 out of its case. I heard Debbie's breath catch in her chest. "No matter how many times I see one of those, I always start to tear up."

"Maybe someday you'll feel that way about me?" I Tom Cruised my best smile at her.

She raised an eyebrow and looked at me like I had three heads. *Okay, then, perhaps not...*

"Can we just stay focused on the mission, please?"

"Roger."

"So what time are we going over to the heroin house?"

"I'm going over about two a.m. You're gonna stay here with Mr. Remington and watch from the front window." I looked at my watch, which read 10:32. "We have some time, wanna take a nap?"

"Here? Are you kidding me? You'll wake up to rats feeding on your toes."

"Yeah, good point. Wanna Barry White instead?"

"Jesus, Jack. This place is gross. Can you please stay focused on the mission, for the umpteenth time?"

"Fine." She was no fun. I crossed my arms and leaned against the wall.

A loud crash came from the apartment next door, and I sighed. "Wait'll I get ahold of that Jimmy the Guinea."

"Seriously? You rented a place from a guy that calls himself Jimmy the Guinea? That's his street name?"

"Yeah, so?"

The crying next door intensified, and I closed my eyes and shook my head. "This is freaking torture. Talk about killing my tranquility."

"Calm down. Why don't you try meditation?"

"How's that going to help?"

A blast that sounded like a gunshot shook the whole house. The screaming stopped and all was quiet. A few seconds later, soft weeping followed, and I stood up and shook my head. "Sorry, babe, I can't put up with this anymore."

"Wait. Jack..."

"You and Saber stay here, I'll be right back."

I drew my Glock and screwed on the silencer. I opened the door, stepped out into the hallway, and tiptoed over to the apartment next to ours. I pushed open the door to 2B.

9

THE DOOR OPENED into a living room that was almost as messy as ours. Same painted plywood floor, but it had more broken furniture. The galley kitchen was off to my left, and like the living room it was empty of people. A hallway ran from the living room towards the back of the unit, and with my Glock leading the way, I inched my way forward.

I approached the first doorway and peeked inside. I hadn't heard anything coming from that room since I'd entered the apartment, so I didn't expect to see anyone inside it. There was a young child lying on the bed, on her stomach, crying softly into a pillow. She looked to be about eight years old, and she was clutching a teddy bear so tight that I could see the veins in her skinny brown arms popping out from the strain. *Jeez, how does a kid get so unlucky that she's born into this mess?*

I slid down the hall and approached the next bedroom.

The door was closed, but not all the way, and I could see movement in the room as I got closer. I looked inside and couldn't believe my eyes.

It was the master bedroom, and it contained a king-size mattress lying on the purple shag carpet. A young lady, maybe in her twenties, was tied up on the sheetless mattress. Her hands were over her head and her ankles were tied to the corners of the mattress. Two men, their backs to the doorway, were kneeling beside her, giggling like schoolkids as they fondled her breasts through her T-shirt. One of the men took out a hypodermic needle and stuck it in her arm, depressing the plunger.

The needle bearer elbowed the other but didn't take his eyes from the lady. "Go get the bitch's daughter. We'll have some fun with her and put it on Facebook. That'll teach Mommy to give us a hard time."

The man stood up and opened the door to leave the room. He bumped right into my Osprey silencer with his forehead. I raised the handle of the Glock an inch or two, pointing it downward in an attempt to keep the bullet inside his body. I hated cleaning up messes.

I pulled the trigger.

An audible "Phfat" silenced the other man's giggles. His partner in crime crumpled to the floor, bullet still inside thank God, and I silently congratulated myself on a brilliant display of cleanliness. How come Debbie was never around to see me shine?

The other man turned his head slowly, as if that would prevent me from shooting him.

It worked. I grabbed him by his ponytail and kneed him in the jaw so hard that he became airborne and flew against the wall, smacking the back of his head with a sickening thud.

I reached down and felt the girl's pulse. It was strong. I looked down at the hypodermic needle the guy had stuck in her arm and saw that it was more than half-full, which was a good sign.

"Ahem."

Oh, crap. I knew Debbie's "ahems" when she was upset, and man, was I in trouble. I turned to face her, an apologetic look on my face. "Sorry, honey."

She stood in the doorway, Glock in one hand, Wonder Woman pose with the other. She shook her head side to side like a disapproving nun at a Catholic grammar school who'd just caught one of the boys peeking up a girl's dress. "Jesus, Jack, what the hell have you done now? You couldn't leave well enough alone, could you?"

"They were going to violate the little girl."

"Can't save the world, Jack. We're here for my sister, remember?"

"Oh, come on, I can't look the other way when it comes to a kid. What kind of man would I be if I did that?"

She pursed her lips and tightened her eyes. She knew I was right. "Fine, but when I get my hands on that Jimmy the Guinea fellow, he's gonna wish he never met you."

"Deal. I'll even let you take the first swing at him. But for now, let's drag these bozos to the basement. Where's Saber?"

"I sent him into the girl's room to keep her company. I think she liked him. He climbed up on her bed to comfort her and licked her face. She stopped crying, made a stink about yucky doggy germs, and wrapped her arms around his neck in a bear hug."

"Can you run downstairs and make sure the front door is locked? Last thing I need is some clown wandering in while we're dragging these hammerheads down to the basement."

"On it." She tucked the Glock into her belt. "You have a key to the basement door?"

"Yeah, it's the same as the front door."

She left and I peeked down the hallway to verify the door to the little girl's room was closed. It was, so I dragged Bullet Boy over to the door of the apartment, admiring my handiwork all the while. If you looked at him quick, you wouldn't even know that he had been shot in the head with a 9mm. A pencil-thin entrance hole dotted the top of his forehead, and the bullet was lodged somewhere inside of him. The perfect shot. He didn't even have any blood coming out of his mouth. I bet they'd study this perfection in coroner's school.

I went back and grabbed the head slammer and pulled him across the floor to the front door. I let him fall next to his buddy and opened the door to peek out into the hallway. Debbie was running up the stairs, taking them two at a time in an impressive athletic form that made me smile. "Door's locked," she said. "Stop staring at my tits, we have work to do."

I was caught again. "Right. I'll take Bullet Boy, you grab the other one."

In a few minutes, we had both bodies next to the steel basement door, without any trace of blood on the stairs. I'm talking zero. This was going to work out perfect. No mess to clean, and by the time anyone stumbled across these bodies, we'd be long gone.

I broke out the front door key, inserted it into the door-knob, and turned it.

It didn't move.

"Shit, the key doesn't work."

"You sure?"

"Yes, I'm sure. How hard could it be to get a key to work?"

"Maybe you just need to jiggle it."

"Still no good. Why don't you go upstairs and check on everyone?"

"Roger." Debbie turned and ran up the stairs. I couldn't help myself and took a break from my key jiggling to watch her.

"Stop staring at my butt."

"I wasn't staring." Right.

I jiggled the key some more, but the lock wouldn't budge. I could break the door down or pry it open, but steel doors are tough as nails, and I hadn't brought any tools for that job. I had my Glock, and I could unlock the door with a couple of well-placed shots, but then I wouldn't be able to lock the door, which meant that the discovery of the decomposed thugs would happen that much sooner.

My thoughts were interrupted by flashing red lights, and my worst nightmare was about to happen. Debbie whisper-yelled down from the second floor. "Jack, the cops are here!"

She came running down the stairs, and we dragged both bodies under the stairwell and laid them one on top of the other so they couldn't be seen from the front entrance. By coincidence, they wound up face-to-face in an intimate embrace. They looked so peaceful, like gay lovers cuddling after a long night of passion.

I pulled out my Glock and waited. This was not how I'd planned on doing things, and the last I wanted was to kill a good guy, but there was no way in hell I was going to get arrested.

During my research, I'd learned that all Newburgh cops wore bulletproof vests. I'd also learned that a 9mm bullet to the solar plexus would be the best way to knock the wind out of them. If that didn't work, well, then, I only had one option left. Hopefully it wouldn't come to that, but if it did...

I could hear the walkie-talkies of the cops as they came up the front steps. We stood on the two bodies and pressed our backs flat against the wall under the staircase to hide. I took out my police scanner. I turned it on, made sure that the volume was on low, and held it against my ear.

Wow, Newburgh was hopping. Dispatch was barking out orders to patrol cars a mile a minute, sounding like an overworked auctioneer. I heard the loud banging of a nightstick against the front door, followed by, "Newburgh Police, open up!"

There was a few-second pause, and when no responses came, the nightstick knocking resumed, this time louder. Fortunately, there was no one else around to open the door and let them in. I knew that the cops wouldn't break the door down unless they heard a gunshot or a cry for help, so I was confident just waiting them out until they left.

I felt the ground shift under my feet and realized that Head Banger was coming around. We stepped off him. He moaned a few times, and his eyes opened. That's all I needed. If he made a ruckus, the cops *would* break the door down. Debbie jammed her silenced Glock against his forehead. She held a finger to her lips to silence the evildoer. Unfortunately, he either didn't understand, or couldn't contain his glee at the sight of such a hot woman hovering so close over him, because he opened his mouth to speak.

Debbie pulled the trigger, caught the ejected shell in her hand, and stuck her Glock in her belt. She volleyballed the shell between her hands a few times until it cooled off, then pocketed it and took out her Glock. God, she's amazing.

After a few more tense minutes and some harried exchanges with the police dispatcher, the officers decided to move on to a live shooter on Grand Street. They hustled back to their squad car and pulled away.

"Whew, that was close," Debbie said. "Did you get the door open?"

"No, freaking key isn't working."

"What's your plan? Can't just leave them here."

I pressed the Glock against where the tongue of the doorknob goes into the door frame. "No other choice." I looked away to protect my face from flying metal, gestured for Debbie to do the same, and squeezed the trigger.

The tongue of the doorknob shattered on impact, and the door creaked slowly open towards me. Debbie bent over and picked up the shell casing. I reached in and found a light switch. A single dim bulb hung from the center of the room and provided just enough light for me to drag the two dead men into the far corner of the damp and moldy basement without tripping over anything.

I sat them up, wrapped their arms around each other's necks, and pressed their lips together.

Debbie giggled. "Jesus, Jack, you're like a freakin' twelve-year-old."

I smiled and started my search for a way to secure the door. Aside from garbage, empty liquor bottles, dirty syringes, and used condoms strewn all over the concrete floor, the only thing in the basement was an old furnace that took up almost half of the room, and a washer and dryer that were so old that they looked like they were models for the original patent application in 1858. I came up empty.

Then it hit me.

"I have to get something. Why don't you go upstairs and keep the young girl company?"

"Okay, but she fell asleep with her arms around Saber's neck. That dog is so freakin' smart. When I opened the door to check on her, he just eyeballed me without moving. It's like he knew that he would wake her up if he raised his head."

"How's the mom?"

"Her pulse is strong and her breathing is good. Hopefully she'll be fine. Do you think we should call an ambulance, just to be on the safe side?"

"Ha, there's a long wait for one of them." I held up the scanner so she understood how I knew. "By the time they get here, she'll either be dead or fine. So no, let's just watch her for a while. If her pulse weakens or she's struggling, we can drop her off at the emergency room. I'm sure that a city like Newburgh has a no-questions-asked policy when you drop off an overdose victim."

I ran upstairs and retrieved my spool of paracord. This stuff was amazing. Only a quarter inch in diameter, and it could hold twelve hundred pounds.

I double-knotted one end over the doorknob on the basement side of the door, and draped it over a large furnace pipe on the basement ceiling about ten feet away. I fed it back under the basement door, pulling on the paracord to take up the slack as I slowly closed it. Once the door was shut tight, I slid the paracord along the bottom of the door and over to the hinged side. I slid it up the side until I encountered the door hinge closest to the floor. I pulled it tight against the bottom of the hinge, knotted it, and cut off the excess. I took out my lighter and melted the knot. I grabbed the doorknob and pulled with all my strength. The door moved less than a quarter of an inch. Nice.

I stepped back and admired my handiwork. Unless you were on your hands and knees and looking right at it, the knot under the bottom door hinge was invisible.

Debbie returned and watched me secure the door without saying a word. When I finished, she let the compliments fly. "That's impressive. There might still be hope for you."

She kissed me on the cheek and gave me a quick hug, then reported on the mom's condition. "I untied Mother and she started coming around. She's groggy and doesn't remember anything."

"Good, less explaining for us. Just tell her that we heard a noise and came over and she was asleep on the bed."

"Already did that."

"She buy it?"

"I think so. There's no reason for us to lie, right? I rescued Saber too. Managed to get him out without waking the girl."

Footsteps came down the stairs and I pushed Debbie under the staircase and out of sight. People might or might not remember my face, but nobody was going to forget hers. Or her body.

The mother appeared on the first-floor landing. Her hair was a mess and she looked a little shaky. Probably still high from the heroin. She looked down the basement steps and made eye contact with me. Her eyes lit up and her mouth opened.

"Hey, it's you?"

"Sorry, ma'am?"

"I saw you, right before I passed out. I thought it was a dream, but it's all coming back to me. You were with those two men." She paused and looked down at the floor. "They used to be my husband's friends, before he died. He was killed in a drive-by four years ago. On the corner of Grant." She looked heavenwards and did the sign of the cross. "Thank you for chasing them away. They stop over every once in a while, uninvited."

"Oh, you're welcome. It was nothing. They ran out as soon as they saw me."

She looked at me and smiled. Her teeth were yellowish brown and had wide gaps between them. "Hey, was that your dog in Yolanda's room?"

"Yeah, but don't worry, he wouldn't hurt her."

"I know he wouldn't. Yolanda looked so peaceful sleeping next to him. Hey, can I keep him?"

"Uhh, no, I'm rather attached to him."

"Okay, but if you change your mind, I'll take him." She paused and cocked her head to one side. "Hey, you my new neighbor? This building's lonely by myself. I can use a man around."

Out of the corner of my eye I saw Debbie shake her head and smack her forehead. It took all my willpower to hold in my smile. "No, I'm just staying for a day or two, sort of a test run to see if I like living here."

"Oh, okay. Well, if you decide to stay here, I'd be happy to have you. This building's good. Except I've been after the landlord to fix the laundry in the basement for months now. He keeps promising that he'll come over and fix it. But he hasn't done it yet. I told him no more sex until he does. But I'm not good at keeping promises."

"Oh, uhm, okay, thanks for that."

"Hey, could you fix it? I have a key to the basement. Want me to get it? Then I can have sex with you instead of the landlord. He's old."

"No, I'm not very handy. At all."

"That's a surprise. Big hunky man like you." She smiled and batted her eyelashes at me.

Debbie drew her Glock, pointed it at the stairs with both hands in a kneeling position, and pretended to empty it into my new best friend.

I stifled a smile. "Oh, I've never been very handy."

I wanted to go up the stairs but didn't want her to think that my closing the distance between us was any kind of invite or show of affection. But I couldn't just stand there all night, so I took a few steps up. I stopped three steps from her and held out my hand. "Well, I'll be going now. Nice chatting with you."

"You too." She grabbed my hand and squeezed hard, holding on for way too long, and took a half step closer to me. "Wow, you have a strong grip. My name's Mariana.

Everyone in our family has a name that ends in A. Hey, you can come by anytime, even if you don't move here." She winked at me, held my gaze, and went up the stairs.

Debbie stepped out from behind the stairs and closed her eyes so tight that she looked like she'd eaten ice cream too fast and gotten hammered with a bad case of brain freeze. "That Jimmy the Guinea is freakin' toast."

"Let's just hope that the landlord doesn't come here anytime soon to fix the laundry in the basement. Otherwise, we'll be leaving in a hurry."

"Hey. Don't worry." She smirked at her Mariana imitation. "Your little *Mariana* will keep screwing him, so he has no incentive to do any work. C'mon, Patrick, *we* have work to do."

I'd had enough of her childish insults and decided to take a stand. "Ya know, you better be nice to me. I bet Mariana would *never* call me a Patrick. *And,* I know for a fact that I could fix her washing machine."

She elbowed me in the gut. "Move it, Patrick."

11
_____

BY THE TIME we got back to the apartment, it was after midnight. I still had some time to kill, and I took Saber out in the backyard and let him sniff around the garbage for a while before going back upstairs. Mariana had music playing, some kind of Spanish dance stuff, and I smelled marijuana when I got to the top of the stairs. I felt sorry for Yolanda, having to grow up in that environment, but there was nothing more I could do for her.

I let myself into our apartment and saw Debbie sitting in the dark by the slightly opened front window, loading the Remington. She had two boxes of shells by her side, along with Saber's bed, two bottles of water, a protein bar, and a pair of night vision binoculars.

She looked at me and nodded. "I'm all set."

"Good. How busy is it?" I asked, in reference to the

heroin house that sat across the street and six houses down from us.

"Not too busy. They have a couple of kids sitting on the front stoop with a pit bull, acting as lookouts and steering the customers around the side to the entrance. Looks like all the action is taking place on the third floor. How are you going in?"

"I'll approach from the rear and blast my way in."

"Subtle."

"Can you think of something better?"

"No, but can't you come up with some fancy ninja quiet James Bond stuff and take 'em out one by one with a karate chop to the neck?"

"Ha, no. But I can shoot them in the head."

"Show-off. What if Catherine's not there? How are you going to find out where she is if they're all dead?"

"This heroin house is run by a guy named Jorge. I memorized his photo. I'll find him and keep him alive until I find her. If she's not there, then I'll cuff him and bring him here to waterboard him. I'll get him to talk, don't worry."

I looked at my watch and saw I still had another thirty minutes before my departure time. I sat down next to her and kissed her on the cheek. "You gonna miss me?"

"Not as long as Saber's by my side." She reached down and stroked his head. "What's your estimated time inside that dump?"

"I'm not sure how long it will take me to gain access, but once I'm inside, it can't be more than five or ten minutes. It's not like I'll be running into any old friends that I haven't seen in years and we wind up chatting over a spoonful of heroin as we catch up on each other's lives."

"I'll be checking you for needle marks when you get back. I better not find any."

"You won't, I promise. I prefer to smoke it. What should I do if I see Mariana there? What if I have to take one for the team to buy her silence?"

"I don't care what you do with her, but no way in hell is she getting Saber."

I looked out the window and down the street, which was dark. The night sky was partly cloudy, and the half moon added a little light to the street when it wasn't obstructed by a passing cloud. Wasn't much, but enough to make my way without a flashlight.

Every single streetlight was out, and none of the homes had any outdoor lighting. "Sure is a pretty dark street. I bet the gangs shoot out any exterior lights that folks put on their houses," I said.

"I don't think too many people live here. Looks like about half the homes are boarded up."

I grabbed my flannel shirt, threw it on over my T-shirt, and gave her a kiss on the lips. "It's go time, baby." She stood up and gave me a hug, holding me extra tight for a long time. She might not have waxed poetic romance phrases about us and tacked them to the fridge, but I could tell that she loved me from her hugs. "I'll be back in a bit, babe. Don't fall asleep on the job." I patted Saber's head and left.

I made my way down the stairs and out the front door into the cool darkness. I made a left turn on the sidewalk and crossed the street before I reached the corner. I pictured Debbie watching me with the night vision binoculars and fought back the urge to moon her. *Jeez, stay freakin' focused!*

We had driven this route a few times in daylight, so I knew exactly where I was going. I turned right at the corner and made my way to Johnson Street, where I made another right. I walked along Johnson until I found the property that backed up to the Landers Street heroin house, and snuck down an alleyway I had found while examining the drone footage Amelia had captured.

The garbage-littered alleyway was only about three feet wide, and the buildings on either side seemed to be abandoned. I hustled through and came up on the eight-foot-high chain-link fence that surrounded the rear of the heroin house property. The three-story brick structure was one of several abandoned properties that were owned by the city. But all they had done was board up the broken windows and put a fence around it with a bunch of graffiti-covered "Keep Out" signs in sun-faded red.

I took out my night vision goggles and scoped out the rear of the house. Other than the garbage and broken furniture that was scattered throughout the backyard, I didn't see anything.

Most of the brick structure was overgrown with ivy, and the weeds and brush in parts of the backyard were almost as tall as I was. I should have brought my machete to chop through it. I wondered how many snakes and spiders I'd be brushing up against and said a silent prayer of thanks that we didn't have any scorpions in this part of the country. At least Newburgh had something good going for it...

I took out my wire cutters and cut an opening large enough that I could squeeze through without leaving any skin behind. I pulled open the fence, which was harder than it sounds, thanks to all the ivy and other plants that had grown around and through it over the years, and shimmied through it.

Once I was in the backyard, I crouched my way through the dense part closest to the fence and stopped just short of a small clearing that was the backyard. Before I stepped out into the open and exposed myself, figuratively speaking of course, I wanted to make sure that the coast was clear.

I knelt down, closed my eyes, and slowed my breathing so that I could absorb all the sounds around me. The crickets were here, but not in great numbers. Music came from inside the heroin house. It was reggae, maybe Bob Marley. Something about no woman and crime, which I didn't quite understand, but a catchy tune nonetheless. A dog bark came from in front of the house, followed by a throaty command to shut the fuck up. Nice way to talk to a dog.

I didn't hear anything that set off my internal alarm, so I stepped out into the clearing, all proud of my silent ninja abilities. Bruce Lee? Pfft. Amateur. Jackie Chan? Yawn. Jason Bourne? Ha, nothing but a twelve-year-old compared to me.

The backyard motion detector picked me up and turned on an exterior light that was so bright that I could be seen from Mars.

12

I HEARD the click of the motion detector and knew right away that I'd done a Patrick. I had my Glock drawn and extinguished the light on my third shot. Less than a second had passed, but the damage had already been done.

Lights came on in what had previously been dimly lit rooms, and three men came rushing out the side door, pistols in hand. One of the men went to the front of the house and came back with a gray pit bull, who was tugging at his leash with a puppyish exuberance. The other two waited for him and then followed him into the backyard. I had already finished chastising my dumb ass, and backed my way into the dense brush. I watched the men through my night vision goggles, Glock at the ready.

They must have had a lot of confidence in this pit bull's tracking ability, because they dropped his leash and let him run circles around the backyard until he found his desired object. A ratty old ball. He grabbed it, shook the mold and dirt off it, and sat down and chewed on it, his tiny tail wagging a mile a minute.

The three men stood there in the dark looking at each other, unsure of what to do next. They looked around over their shoulders, waited a few minutes, and then shrugged at each other before deciding to head back inside.

My escape was pure luck. If they had been halfway competent, or had a worthier guard dog, I would have been discovered. I had no qualms about shooting the three—in fact, I'd almost done so right there—but I struggled with shooting a dog, especially after my hero, London, had taken a bullet for my Debbie.

After waiting another ten minutes to make sure no one else came out of the house, I stood up, my knees creaking in revolt at kneeling for so long. I walked out into the clearing and over to the rear corner of the house. Peering around it, I saw what must have been a three-hundred-pound mountain of a man, bald and bearded, standing guard by the side door.

I decided I should try and find another way into the house.

Amelia's aerial footage had uncovered a cellar door, the kind that lies on the ground at an angle, on the opposite side of the house. It probably hadn't been used in decades, and by all rights should have been locked. I tiptoed over to it, pushed my hand through the ivy and searched for the handle. I found it and gave it a tug. It didn't budge. It must have been locked, or maybe just rusted shut. I yanked on it harder, and the handle snapped off, sending me tumbling backwards into the weeds. I jumped to my feet, swatted through a spiderweb, and fought my way through the brush and back into the yard.

At least I was on the side of the house that Debbie couldn't see. Otherwise, I'd never live that one down. I still had the rusty handle in my grip, so I tossed it in the weeds.

I studied that side of the house but saw no other way to get in. I was out of options. Looked like it would be access through the side door mountain man for me.

I tiptoed back across the backyard and peeked around the corner. Mountain Man was talking to a young lady, trying to impress her no doubt, as he rolled up one leg of his oversized shorts and explained to her the origin of his King Cobra thigh tattoo that started at his gigantic calf, which was as wide as a football.

The two jawed for a few minutes and the girl finally tired of his spiel, so she said goodbye and turned and walked away. I had already made up my mind on how I was going to kill Mountain Man, but the real challenge was what to do with his massive body. If I just left it on the sidewalk, he'd be spotted quicker than a beached whale on Fourth of July weekend in the Hamptons, so I had to make him disappear.

Seeing him focused on the young girl's ass as she strutted away, complete with a few *mmm, mmm, mmm*s, gave me my opening. I snuck up behind him. As the girl disappeared around the front corner of the house, he adjusted his crotch. I leapt on him, snaked my right arm under his double chin, and locked in a rear naked choke around his tree-sized neck.

Before Mountain Man knew what hit him, I leaned him backwards. To keep himself from falling backwards, he windmilled his arms and backstepped in sync with me. Right into the backyard. My rear naked choke hold on his arteries was so tight that I felt him go limp a few times. I didn't want to have to drag his big ass, so I let off on the pressure for a few seconds. He'd start to come around, and I'd reapply the pressure, causing him to fade out again. We repeated our dance a few times until we reached the dense foliage against the backyard fence, where I put him down for good.

I had already pissed away three bullets on the motion detection light and didn't feel like wasting any more, but this needed to look like a gang war. I rolled him over to his belly, waited for the grogginess to wear off for the medical examiner's sake, and shot him twice in the back of his head. *Twelve bullets left.*

I left the cover of the underbrush and trotted over to the side door. I cracked the door and looked inside. It led to a stairway that went up to the left, or down to the right into the basement. The basement was dark, so I chose to go left, which put me in an empty kitchen. The place smelled like you would imagine an abandoned home retrofitted into a heroin house would smell like. Old and moldy, with marijuana and heroin odors wafting about.

The kitchen led to a living room that had a single couch against the wall. A couple were making out on the couch, and I caught sight of an AR-15 leaned up against the side of the couch. The guy was a skinhead, shirtless and covered with tattoos and gold chains.

Someone stumbled down the stairs and interrupted the makeout man on the couch to ask him if he could use the bathroom. He was met with a gruff, "No, this ain't a gas station. You got what you came for, so do your dirty business somewhere else." What a douche bag. The denied customer slouched at the shoulders and shuffled out the front door past the two teenagers and the hard-at-work pit bull, who was rolling around the front yard, happier than a pig in shit, destroying his new toy.

There was no way around the AR-15 guy and his chick, so I shot him twice in the chest. She was so stoned she didn't even realize what happened. I rear naked choked her out, the effects of which would wear off in a few seconds, and when she came to she'd have no permanent damage, so I tied her hands behind her back with her late lover's belt and stuck a piece of duct tape over her mouth. I had a phobia about taping an innocent person's mouth shut and them dying because they had a head cold and couldn't breathe through their nose, so I bent down to listen to her breathing. She'd be fine. I slid the couch back away from the wall and tossed the dead guy on the floor. I laid her on top of him.

I emptied the AR-15 and did a quick disassemble that would have made Debbie proud. Except that my eyes were open. I pocketed the bolt carrier group, making the rifle useless. I hid it under the couch and turned off the lamp on the end table. I tossed it behind the couch, careful not to whack the girl.

I made my way over to the stairs and took a deep breath. This was it, showtime. The shit was gonna hit the fan in about twenty seconds. I took another deep breath, grabbed the railing with my right hand, and...

"Hey! Where's Dominic? And who the fuck are you?"

Shit.

13

I TURNED SLIGHTLY to my right, just enough to bring my left hand across my belly, but still hidden by my open flannel shirt. I hated this with a passion, but I had no choice. I fired blindly, two quick shots through my favorite flannel, praying to God that I hit the bastard and didn't put holes in my shirt for nothing. *Eight bullets left.*

I heard the solid thunks of bullets hitting fleshy mass, and turned all the way around to see him collapse to his knees. His eyes were wide open, and blood dripped from his mouth. He wobbled for a second and face-planted with a loud smack of forehead against floor. His pistol lay at his feet.

Goddamnit, another freaking body to get rid of. I hated this shit. I hustled over, stuffed his gun in my pocket, and grabbed him by the feet. I pulled him down the stairs to the basement, leaving a trail of blood from the two exit wounds in the middle of his back, and dropped him next to the stairs. I kicked him in the nuts, payback for making me put two holes in my shirt. I'd been practicing that move for years, and never, not one freaking time, did I ever manage to put the second shot through the hole created by the first one. #Freakincursed.

I hauled ass back to the kitchen, into the living room, and up the stairs, taking them two at a time. Enough fooling around.

I reached the top of the stairs and stepped into a hallway. To the left were two rooms, their doors removed, and to the right was one open doorway. The two rooms on the left were dimly lit, both with music coming out of them. With my Glock leading the way, I moved to the first room and stepped inside. It was empty.

I went to the second room and found four people sitting on a couch, getting high. The guy closest to me reached for his pistol and I shot him in the face. *How many bullets left? Shit, lost count...* The others were in shock, but that wore off fast. I creamed the second guy across the temple with my Glock, and he toppled off the couch and hit the coffee table facefirst, collapsing the legs on one side of it. His face slid down leaving a trail of blood, until it came to a stop against the floor.

I checked out the two girls. They couldn't have been more than twenty, but they looked like crap. Dark circles under their eyes, oily hair, and overall unkempt appearance that had me shaking my head.

"Close your eyes." I pointed my gun at them. "What are your names?"

"Sofia." "Maria." They blurted them out at the same time, followed by sniffles.

What's with all the names ending in A in this freakin' town?

"Any other ladies here?"

"No. Please don't shoot us."

"Shut up. One more word and I will. Now put your hands together."

They did, each of them trembling, and I cable-tied them together. I took out the duct tape and put a piece on each of their mouths. I wrapped a piece around their eyes and leaned over and whispered in their ears.

"If you stay here and keep quiet, you might live through this. Understand?"

They both nodded.

The face-plant guy started to move and he let out a groan. I looked down and noticed a small pistol in his belt. I shot him and took his pistol. It was an old ratty no-name semiautomatic with a rusty grip. I unloaded it, broke it down, and pocked the slide.

I popped the ammo magazine out of my Glock and inserted a fresh one. I left the two ladies and made my way down the hall to the front room. I walked through the doorway, and was greeted by a Tina Turner tune, clouds of drug smoke, and a buff security guard seated at a table and texting on his phone.

Before he looked up, he announced my entrance fee: "Twenty dollars."

I'd learned early on in my aviation training that complacency was a killer, and no matter what your occupation, you couldn't take things for granted. Buff security guard took for granted that I had been vetted at the door, and his hesitation to put his phone down and raise his eyes was textbook complacent behavior. Not that it mattered, I mean he was dead anyway, but I loved a challenge. I pointed my Glock at him. "Seriously? Twenty dollars? You charge an entrance fee for people to come in here and buy drugs?"

He looked up, open-mouthed and wide-eyed, and I shot him in the forehead. *Sixteen bullets left.*

I was in the zone, so tightly focused that nothing else mattered. The world could have ended and I wouldn't have noticed. Everything slowed to a crawl. I felt like the Flash.

The room was three times the size of the other two rooms and was lined with couches on three sides, with an occasional floor lamp thrown in between them. Each couch had a beat-up coffee table in front of it that contained various drug paraphernalia and some beer cans.

The couch to my left had a passed-out body curled up on it. A man, I think. I let him be. The couch in front of me had four young men who were sharing a joint. They were wobbling and giggling like they were stoned out of their minds. When they saw me, they turned their heads sideways, like a confused dog, and moved their heads backward and forward as if trying to get me in focus.

None of them were Jorge.

The couch to the right of me had two men sitting on it, one standing in front of it, and another kneeling down and sucking the cock of one of the seated men. I recognized Jorge right away. He sat there with his eyes closed, one hand on the back of the little cocksucker's head, the other holding a cigarette. He let out a few moans and his body started to tense up, the telltale signs of a guy just about ready to finish.

I knew right away that this image had already seared my corneas and that I'd be seeing it forever at the most inappropriate times. *Jeez, the things I do for Debbie.*

I shot the guy standing with his back to me—*fifteen bullets left*—the guy on the couch next to Jorge, and finally the little cocksucker that was kneeling between Jorge's legs. His body started a death quiver, and Jorge took it as a sign of a special oral technique, and he let the guy know how much he appreciated it.

"Yes. That's it. Don't stop!"

The little cocksucker finally finished his death dance and slid to the floor. Jorge started shooting his load, and when the little cocksucker's mouth slipped off his penis, he opened his eyes to see what was going on. In between jets of cum that were shooting impressively high, we made eye contact.

I smiled. His eyes widened when he saw the Glock, and he grabbed his penis, which was shrinking faster than a bank account of one of Bernie Madoff's clients, and shoved it in his cum-drenched Levi's.

"Hi, Jorge. Don't mind me if we don't shake hands." I pressed the silencer against his forehead. "Stand up, turn around, and put your hands behind your fucking head." His bug eyes were blinking a mile a minute, and he looked like an ugly version of *I Dream of Jeannie* trying to blink away a nightmare. Which I was. His worst of course.

He stood up and his pants slid down to his ankles. *Jeez.* "Pull up your pants, you fucking idiot." He bent over, his puckered brown eye winked at me and he farted. He farted. In. My. Face. That bastard. I almost puked.

He yanked up his pants, and this time I gave him enough time to fasten them, which took him a while because his hands were trembling.

I whistled along with Tina's "Private Dancer" and looked around to make sure that no one else was a threat. They weren't. The sleeping beauty on the couch on the left was still out like a light. The four stoned guys on the center couch were now completely passed out. Lucky for them, they were so out of it that they wouldn't remember a thing.

Jorge finished buckling up his creamed-on jeans, and I pushed his face against the wall, put his hands behind his back, and cable-tied them together, careful not to touch any more of him than I needed to. I duct-taped his eyes. There was a camo backpack next to where he was sitting. I grabbed it and unzipped it. It contained cash and bags of white powder. I zipped it shut again, slung it over my shoulder, and led him into the hallway. "We're going for a little walk."

I stopped when we got to the top of the stairs and pushed him against the wall. "Don't move or I'll shoot you." He didn't.

I stepped into the room with the two ladies. They were still sitting on the couch. "Listen up, ladies. Today's your lucky day, because we're not going to kill you." I softly took the duct tape off their mouths and cut through their cable ties, but I left the eye tape on.

"You be sure and tell everyone that OFWGs are in charge now. They leave this hood, or die. Understood? OFWGs, baby."

They turned their heads toward me, foreheads furrowed, and asked, "OFWGs? What's that?"

This was probably my proudest moment of the day. I managed to answer without laughing. "Old Fuckin' White Guys. We're taking back the hood."

Though they still had duct tape over their eyes, they turned and looked at each other...

I left the room and grabbed Jorge by the elbow. "Let's go. We got some steps coming up, so look alive."

We negotiated the stairs without incident, the whole time listening to the girls upstairs curse in pain as they tried to take the duct tape off each other's eyelids. Maybe duct-taping their eyes shut hadn't been such a good idea. More like a Patrick moment. I made a mental note not to mention my lack of taping etiquette to Debbie.

We made it to the bottom of the stairs without incident and made a left. I could still hear the girls. They were crying now, bawling their eyes out. Maybe it was their strategy to wet the tape to loosen it up...

I led Jorge to the side door and we exited the house. I noticed that there were no lights on in the front exterior of the house, so I sat Jorge down and put on my night vision binoculars. I crept up to the front corner and peeked around the side of the house. Nothing. Except the pit bull, who was rolling around in the small patch of grass, chewing on his ball. I looked up and saw that the porch light over the door was shattered. That was a nice coincidence, since I could now walk Jorge to my apartment right down the street, instead of taking the back way, which was a lot longer and presented the added risk of spiders in that overgrown jungle of a backyard. God, I hate spiders.

I went back and retrieved Jorge, who was by now stifling sobs. I walked him down the street and up the steps to our apartment house. Debbie met us at the front door and let us in. Once we were inside the apartment, she let me have it.

"What the hell took you so long?"

"Sorry, babe, it got complicated."

"And who the hell is that?"

"Jorge. Remember? We need to get info from him about Catherine."

"Not him, Patrick, that!"

She pointed behind me, and there was Pit Bull, ball in

mouth, mini tail wagging a mile a minute. The little bugger had followed me home.

I caught a lightning flash of black behind Debbie, and Saber lunged through the air at Pit Bull.

Oh shit...

14

SABER LANDED on him full force, sending him reeling sideways and into the wall with a solid thud that shook the
house. Pit Bull spat out the ball and turned to face Saber. In
one quick motion, faster than I've ever seen anything move
in my life, Saber lunged forward, snatched the ball, and tore
ass into the bedroom. I could swear I heard him laughing.
Pit Bull stood there, stunned, looked at us for a second, and
then chased after Saber.

The two of them wrestled about, chasing each other and
playing with that damn moldy ball all night, as if they were
best friends for life. I'm talking hours of endless frolicking,
with barely a break, until they finally passed out from
exhaustion and fell asleep in Saber's bed.

Jorge didn't have quite as much fun that night. To start
off with, he was paracorded to a chair. Plus, he still had duct
tape over his eyes, which Debbie caught on to right away.

"Jeez, Jack, you trying to pull his eyelids off? That's grue-some, I don't want any part of that. You ever see a guy with no eyelids? It's gross!"

"No, but thanks for the visual."

"What's that all over his pants?"

"Ugh, you don't want to know, just don't touch it." *Damn woman doesn't miss a thing...*a vision of the little cocksucker spasming in death and Jorge's load-shooting prowess, along with his brown stinkeye winking at me, popped into my head. I cringed.

"You okay?"

"Yeah, I'll be fine. Just a tough night, that's all."

"If you want to talk about it..."

Dear God, no.

"No, no, that's okay. I'm good."

"You got nailed by the motion detector, didn't you?"

Damnit. She really doesn't miss a freaking thing.

"Yep, but I shot the lights out right quick." I stuck my chest out in pride at my expert marksmanship. "Just call me Wyatt Earp."

"You missed on every shot."

"What?" I frowned at her. "What are you talking about? All the lights went out."

"That's because I sent a round into the light above the side door. After you left, I studied Amelia's video and I saw that there was a motion detector in the backyard. I saw a conduit pipe running to it from the light above the side door. I had no way to warn you, so I waited with scope on target while you were dicking around the neighborhood. As soon as the light came on, I shot the light fixture over the side door and severed the feed to the motion detector and backyard light."

"What? No way. I'm sure I hit that light."

"Fine. We'll send Amelia over tomorrow to get a damage assessment," She held her hand out. "I bet you five bucks that the backyard lightbulb is still intact."

I shunned her shake and turned serious. "We don't have time for this nonsense. Let's quit fooling around and get to work on Jorge."

We questioned him relentlessly about Catherine, but all he would tell us was that she was fine and hanging with a guy named Roberto.

I led Debbie to the bedroom and closed the door. "I'm losing my patience with this clown. Time to get serious."

I opened up my go bag and took out the sodium pentothal. I loaded up a syringe and went back into the living room. I didn't bother alcohol-swabbing Jorge's arm. I just stabbed him with the needle and drove the plunger all the way home. He jumped and stifled a groan through gritted teeth, having been forewarned that if he screamed, our red-meat-loving Doberman would bite his nuts off.

I waited a few minutes for the truth serum to kick in and started questioning him again. Most of the things we asked him got the same answers, but we did get out of him that Roberto was a fellow drug dealer and that he had been "loaned" Catherine from a drug dealer named Cosmo in

New Jersey. He and Roberto shared Catherine, and she was the best lay he'd ever had, and her tits were freaking gigantic, and he loved her and wanted to marry her, but he needed to talk with Cosmo because she was his, and he wasn't sure how Catherine felt about him, but he would move the earth for her, and he loved her gigantic tits, and he'd slept with hundreds if not thousands of whores, and Catherine was the best by far, and his dying wish was to take his last breath between her humongous tits, and...

I had to duct-tape his mouth to get him to shut up.

I also had to stop Debbie from shooting him on four separate occasions.

After spilling his guts, Jorge passed out, and Debbie and I went over our plan. I picked up Jorge's phone and read through the texts. I found a conversation from Roberto that mentioned Catherine and included a selfie of him next to her. Naked. I looked at the photo longer than what was polite and turned my back so that Debbie couldn't see it. She'd had enough bad news for one night.

I thought long and hard before putting my plan into action, and I texted Roberto from Jorge's phone.

Jorge: u round dog?

Roberto: what up dude?

Jorge: need some shit

Roberto: now? its late dude

Jorge: make it worth your while. Big client

Roberto: oh why didn't you say so? Meet me in 30 at the usual

Jorge: naw man, bad news at the house, let's do the ware-house on liberty

Roberto: see you in 30

I turned off the phone and looked at Debbie. "We're on. Let's go. Grab your weapons, I need you as top cover."

"Roger. Where are we going?"

"Warehouse on Liberty." I knew from my HFS research that they used an abandoned warehouse at that location to conduct business.

We grabbed our bags, took Jorge by the elbow and led him out to the truck. The truth serum was staring to wear off, and he started asking questions. I'd had enough of him, so I got behind him, slid my right arm under his chin, and rear naked choked him out. I held the choke for about thirty seconds longer then needed, in hopes that he would stay out for the short trip. I tossed him into the bed of my Toyota, where he landed with a savage face-plant. I didn't mean to hurt him like that, but when he started falling awkwardly, I reached out to grab him but had to avoid touching the front of his pants at all cost, so I whiffed on the rescue.

Debbie picked up on that. "Nice catch."

We drove down to the Hudson River and I parked by an abandoned pier. I dragged Jorge down to the end and he started to come to, so I rear naked choked him out again. I yanked the duct tape from his eyes, which made him writhe in pain even though he was out cold. I knew I shouldn't have done this, but, I looked at the piece of duct tape before

I balled it up and threw it in the Hudson. I saw his torn-off eyelids on it. My stomach tightened and I almost retched.

I cut the cable ties from his wrists, stuffed a bag of white powder from his backpack into his front pocket, and slid him into the slow-moving Hudson, careful not to look into his eyes.

He floated for a while, and when he reached the middle of the river, he started to come to. He thrashed and screamed in pain, so loud that he awakened the occupants of a moored fishing boat in the Hudson. He disappeared for a minute and then came to the surface.

Like in a bad dream, I watched in slow motion as the lights of the boat flicked on. Someone came on deck, turned on the spotlight and lit up Jorge, his eyeballs reflecting the light like a cartoon monster. He went under, then resurfaced a few yards away. They sounded an air horn, pulled up anchor, and raced over to him.

Before they reached him, he went under for the final time.

15

WE PULLED into the parking lot of the abandoned ware-house on the bank of the Hudson River, and I hopped out and went over to one of the back doors. I picked the lock and let myself in.

Debbie pulled the Toyota into a dark corner of the lot and parked next to a bunch of abandoned vehicles. She was far away but had an unobstructed view of our meeting place, which was the main office just off the side entrance to the warehouse. I couldn't use that entrance because Roberto had installed a massive padlocked chain on it, effectively claiming the warehouse for himself, and I didn't want him to know that I was inside already.

It was dark, but the sun was just peeking over the mountains, so enough light came in through the filthy windows and bird-shit-covered skylights, that I could make my way to the side entrance without walking into anything. I found a dark corner and waited for Roberto.

A few minutes later, Roberto's SUV pulled up and he got out carrying a bag. He looked around and then pulled out a key chain and unlocked the monstrous padlock. The loud ratcheting of the chain as he pulled it free of the door echoed through the warehouse. He tossed the chain on the ground and stepped inside.

He walked over to a desk and put the bag down. I stepped out from the shadows: "Hands up or I shoot."

He did as instructed and turned around to face me. "Who the fuck are you, and where is Jorge?"

"Don't worry about Jorge. Where's Catherine?"

"Catherine? That's what this is about? She's gone, man, back to New Jersey."

I sensed the men before I heard them, and by then it was too late. The unmistakable feeling of the cool metal barrel of a pistol pressed against the back of my neck, and Roberto put his hands down. He reached into his bag and pulled out a pistol. Someone reached around me and grabbed my gun and wrenched it from my hand.

A chair was slid across the floor and I was pulled into it from behind. A hood was pulled over my head, and my hands were tied together behind the chair. My ankles were fastened to the chair legs, and I felt a pair of beefy hands patting me down a little too rough, especially when he reached my nutsack, which made me wince in pain. He held my junk for a couple of seconds more than was necessary to confirm that I didn't have a sawed-off shotgun in my pants, and I heard him giggle at my discomfort.

I tried to appear calm, but inside my heart raced. I had a lot of faith in Debbie, but this was bad, and I had no idea if they'd compromised her position or not. I needed to think fast on my feet if I was going to survive.

"Now, suppose you tell me what this is all about." Roberto's voice was soft and calm, as if we were having a conversation over Sunday brunch at the Hilton.

"Cosmo sent me to look after Catherine. He hadn't heard from her in a while, and he wanted to make sure that she was all right."

"Really," Roberto said. "Hmm, I wonder why Cosmo didn't ask me that himself when he picked her up this morning..."

Shit.

The hood was torn from my head, and Roberto's face was inches from mine. He stank of stale body odor, and it took all my willpower not to gag and cough in his face. He stuck his pistol under my chin. "Quit fucking around, white boy. Why are you looking for Catherine?"

I decided on another tack. "I'm a federal agent."

"Got ID?"

"No, I'm undercover."

"You're full of shit. Enough with the pleasantries." Roberto nodded to one of the guys behind me, probably my ham-fisted nutsack-squeezing buddy, and I heard a knife being drawn from its sheath. Someone knelt down to the right of me, placed their arm around my shoulder and brought me in close, my head resting against his smelly armpit. He placed the blade against my neck, and I felt my skin part under the pressure.

"Hey boss, do a selfie to add to my collection."

"You're a sick fuck Ernesto, you know that?"

Okay, Debbie, love of my life. Now would be a good time to—

The beautiful sound, music to my ears, of glass being punctured by a 2800-feet-per-second projectile never got old. The solid thunk of metal smashing bone was a close second, and my knife-holding nut-squeezing tormentor froze in place for a split second before falling away. I felt the air pressure change as the bullet screamed by my head and ripped through his chest, creating a firehose of blood that painted the right side of my body. Gross.

Her next shot was a head shot. I could tell by the sound of the third guy's head exploding behind me. Thankfully, all his blood and bone fragments were sent sailing in another direction.

You should have seen the look on Roberto's face. A mix of shock, fear, and dread, all captured in a statuesque frozen-in-time second before he blinked himself back to reality. The proverbial Kodak moment.

He spun around to face the window, and his gun hand

disappeared in a cloud of red mist. The gun flew across the concrete floor, clanked off a steel support beam, and continued like an out-of-control fidget spinner on steroids until it hit the back wall of the warehouse.

Roberto crashed to his knees, grasped his right stump, and fell headfirst into the fetal position. He screamed at the top of his lungs for a good fifteen seconds, a high-pitched whining affair that grated on me like fingernails on a chalkboard. He finally passed out from the pain, much to my auditory relief.

I looked around to make sure that there were no more bad guys. I didn't see any.

I shook and pried my hands free just as Debbie came running through the front door. She took one look at me and frowned. "Jeez. You're a mess."

"Yeah, thanks to you." I pointed to a small red mass on the floor that was still pulsing out blood. It was Ernesto's heart, minus a few chunks that had been blasted away.

Debbie stepped over and examined it. "Wow, it's still beating. That's crazy. I wish I had my iPhone with me so I could video it. No one's ever going to believe this."

"I'm telling you right now, I'm not cleaning that shit up. And by the way, that bullet came awful close to my head. I actually felt the air pressure change. Why didn't you do a head shot? Show-off." I continued untying my ankles to free myself from the chair.

She pointed to the third guy, now a headless corpse with blood from his neck spilling out and widening the surrounding pool to over ten feet in diameter, with no signs of slowing down.

"That guy's making even more of a mess. You better get up off your ass. The red blob's coming for you."

I stood up and hopped away from the red sea, then sat back down and finished untying myself. When I was finally free of the chair, I stood back up and noticed that the whole right side of my body was damp, covered in blood from my nutsack-squeezing friend. I couldn't wait for it to dry so it could chafe my skin with every movement. It's a damn shame that killing is a dirty business. Almost takes the fun out of it. I vowed to figure out a cleaner way.

Debbie explained her chest shot rationale. "I couldn't do a head shot because he had a knife at your throat. I had to stop the action. Ever see a chicken running around after its head's been cut off? Well I have, but I've never seen one run around after its heart's been exploded."

"Oh, okay. Well, that makes sense. Thanks for that."

"For my explanation, or for saving your ass again?"

"Both."

"You can make it up to me later. Get any info on Catherine?"

"It appears that she departed for New Jersey."

Debbie grimaced and did an exaggerated full-body shiver. "Jersey? What the heck? Why would she go there?" She pointed an imaginary gun at her temple and finger-clicked a round off. "Just kill me now."

"Be nice, now. It's not so bad." I thought of Cheryl and

Princeton, where I'd first met her at that Italian eatery. I flashed back to her condo, where we'd had that great dinner on one of our first dates, and smiled.

Debbie caught on and frowned. "Sorry, Jack, I wasn't thinking. It just came out..." She touched my left arm, the one without Ernesto's drying blood caked all over it.

"That's okay, baby."

"So now what? What should we do with these guys?" She nodded to the heartless one and his headless compadre. "We shouldn't just leave them here. Some innocent person might stumble across them and be scarred for life."

"I noticed a few empty fifty-gallon drums when I was walking through the warehouse. Want to just drum them up and roll them in the Hudson?"

"Let's do it. You get the drums, I'll pick up the pieces. I know how much you dislike that..."

"Yeah, thanks." I jogged over to get the fifty-gallon metal containers. When I returned with the first one, we picked up the heartless one and folded him into the barrel. At one point in the lifting process, I feared that he might come apart, leaving Debbie and me looking at each other, each holding a half. But the bands of skin holding the two halves together held, and I felt relief as I compressed his upper half on top of his legs in the barrel.

I attached the top of the drum by bending over the tabs, but left them loose so that the barrel would fill up with water and sink. Last thing I wanted was for this thing to float down the Hudson River and bump up against someone's party boat.

I retrieved the second barrel, and we dumped the headless one into it, ahem, headfirst. Once I had the top loosely fastened, we rolled them out the back door, down the handicap ramp, and into the Hudson River. They floated for a while and then disappeared.

We headed back to the warehouse. "What about Roberto?" Debbie asked. "Think he has any more info on Catherine?"

"He's got to. Hopefully we can wake him. I'll shoot him up with the truth serum if we have to."

Debbie grimaced. "Oh God, is he going to nonstop profess his love for Catherine and her gigantic tits too? I don't know if I can handle any more of that. Men are so freaking weak... except you, of course. Dear." She elbowed me in the side, a love tap if there ever was one.

When we got back inside the warehouse and walked to the front, a police car pulled up and two officers got out. They entered through the side entrance with their guns drawn.

Debbie darted to her left, and I to my right, to hide behind some shelving. In my haste to get behind cover, I tripped over some garbage and crashed into a stack of plastic pallets, knocking them over. They crashed down and made enough noise to wake the dead. I whacked my head pretty good, and must have been out of it for a minute or two.

When I looked up, I saw the two cops standing over me, their guns pointed at my face.

16

COSMO REACHED over and placed his hand on Catherine's thigh. "So how'd my lady do up in Newburgh?"

"Eh, it was okay. Roberto and Jorge run a pretty tight ship. Do I think they're skimming some cash off the top? Probably, but if they are, it's not much, and they kept me well fed and supplied me with good shit."

"How was the sex?" He inched his hand higher up her thigh. She really wasn't in the mood, but she spread her legs a little wider to allow easy access. Cosmo liked to be in control, and as long as she let him have his way, he took good care of her.

"Good. I kept them happy, just like you told me."

"That's why you're my number one girl. You know that, right?"

"Of course I do."

She felt Cosmo's fingers touch her, and she closed her

eyes and sighed. She was still wet from her last time with Roberto, and Cosmo inserted a meaty finger and noticed right away. "Wow, you're ready for action, aren't you?"

She opened her eyes and smiled at him. "I'm always ready for you, Cosmo." She undid his pants, reached in with two hands, and tugged him out. She swung a leg over and straddled him. In one smooth motion she slid all the way down on him, a deep groan of pleasure spilling from her lips. She wrapped her arms around his neck and kissed him.

She rode him hard as the big Cadillac SUV did ninety down the New Jersey Turnpike, her ponytail brushing against the roof of the vehicle with each thrust. When she felt him tense up, she climbed off and took him in her mouth. She swallowed every drop, devouring him like a gourmet meal. Cosmo liked that.

She waited a few minutes, gently put him back, and zipped him up. He opened his eyes, took out a joint and gave it to her. She lit up, and after the first few tokes, the pain went away.

Life was good.

17

"FREEZE, MOTHERFUCKER! DON'T MOVE!" the male cop screamed so loud my ears hurt. He looked like he was wired on too much Red Bull. I tried to lighten the mood with some levity.

"Easy, son, you'll have a stroke," I said.

He didn't seem to appreciate my humor. He screamed even louder this time: "Put your fuckin hands in the air!"

"Hold on now, son. Do I freeze, or put my hands in the air? Which one is it?"

Debbie finally arrived. Thank God I wouldn't have to deal with this clown anymore. Nothing worse than someone who doesn't appreciate a sense of humor.

She called out to them. "Hey!"

They turned and she fired twice. I could tell by the way they folded in half and flew backwards that she nailed them both in the solar plexus, and I knew by the sound of bullets hitting Kevlar that they both had their vests on. I still felt bad for them. Getting shot, vest or not, hurt like hell.

When the male cop got hit, he squeezed off a round into the concrete by his feet, and I got peppered in the face with flying chunks of cement. I knew enough to close my eyes when Debbie called to them, so at least my sight was saved.

My hearing didn't fare as well. The non-silenced gunshot inside the cavernous building rattled my eardrums so hard that I couldn't hear anything aside from a loud ringing noise. I saw Debbie come over and pick up their guns. She said something, but I didn't hear anything, which was scary.

The two cops rolled around on the floor, holding their stomachs, agony all over their faces. Debbie's perfectly placed shots had succeeded in rendering them harmless, without hurting them permanently. I'd been kicked in the solar plexus in a Tae Kwon Do tournament once, and man, did that hurt. My whole body had shut down and I couldn't breathe for five seconds, enough time for my adversary to pummel me and have the ref step in to stop it. I couldn't imagine how much a bullet, vest or not, must have hurt.

We sat them up and used their own handcuffs to secure their hands behind their backs. When they started to come to, I explained the situation to them.

"We're special agents with the FBI, working undercover," I lied. "You stumbled into something way over your pay grade."

The male spoke first. "I don't believe you. Why would you shoot us? Where's your ID?"

The female added: "You could have killed us."

I didn't have any time or patience for this, so I took their IDs and went out to my truck. I opened my iPad, logged in to TOR, and searched them on HFS.

In ten minutes I had enough info on them, so I went back into the warehouse.

I started with the man. "Here's the deal, Juan Pablo Escobar," I said, using his video game screen name. "Your wife isn't cheating on you, yet. But you better start paying attention to her, or she will. And you don't have to worry about that fellow Chuck that she works with. He's gay. Your daughter missed her period, which is why she's been so cranky the past few weeks. Your son has been watching porn on RedTube. His favorite categories are threesomes with MILFs, and amateur pegging, but I'd guess that's just a phase he's going through.

"Your wife's favorite category is just one-on-one fucking, a little on the rough side. Smack her ass once in a while. She loves when you do that from behind, but she's reluctant to admit it because she feels that you don't respect her wants, which is why she's, ahem, let's just say on the verge of an anonymous Tinder account.

"Your promotion didn't come through because your sergeant has it in for you, ever since you made that comment about 'fat chicks need loving too' while you

Michael Jackson'ed your crotch seven weeks ago. His daughter is overweight."

His mouth opened so far I could see his tonsils.

His female partner just looked at him, as if trying to figure out if anything I said was true. His silence proved it was.

"And you, ma'am. Your son Pedro's a great kid. He's just going through some tough teen years, no father figure and all. I know he's all you have, but you've got to let him go to Dartmouth. No more of that 'oh, it's so far away' crap. Their engineering program is a perfect fit for him, and he really wants that. He needs that. He hasn't told you that yet, but mark my words, he has his heart set on that scholarship. And his friend Andrew, the one who's so polite and prim and proper? The one you really like? He's a pot head. He deals on the side—not big amounts, but he's a borderline felon if he gets caught. You don't want Pedro hanging out with him anymore. And that guy you've been chatting with online—what's his screen name again? 'Great to be with me 69' or something like that? He's been married three times before he turned forty. He's not a good fit for you. I know he's a great talker and all, but he's cheated in every relationship that he's ever had. And he doesn't even have an IRA."

The two cops sat there, stunned. They looked at me, then at each other, then back to me. The silence was deafening, so I continued.

"So here's how this plays out. Roberto over there is a big-time drug dealer. You guys caught him in the act of dealing, and a shoot-out ensued. The others got away, but you recovered heroin, weapons, and cash. Capiche?"

The two of them looked at each other again. I opened the backpack and tossed a few bags of heroin at them. Then some stacks of twenties. Then a few more.

I kept tossing heroin and cash at them until I saw their eyes light up, and I knew I had them. Never mind this "you had me at hello" stuff. I had them at multiple pounds of heroin, tens of thousands in cash, and certain promotions, along with cushy job assignments in the Newburgh Police Department.

I told them how Roberto had killed two men tonight and stuffed them in fifty-gallon drums and tossed them in the Hudson. I let on that Roberto also killed Jorge. By the end of their shift, they had arrested a one-handed drug dealer who'd killed three people in cold blood, and recovered millions of dollars in heroin and tens of thousands in cash. #Heroes

Debbie and I showed the two cops the handcuff keys that we'd left by the back warehouse door. All they had to do was make it to the back door, grab the keys, and unlock each other's cuffs, and they were home free. And we'd be long gone.

I heard their chairs sliding across the concrete as we left.

18

BY THE TIME we got back to our apartment, it was daylight, but I wasn't worried about being spotted anymore. We knew our stay at Newburgh was over. I did a quick change of clothes, and without a word between us, we tossed all of our bags into the bed of the Toyota. We decided to keep the pit bull puppy, who I named Buddy, and after letting the two dogs in the backyard to take care of business, we put them in the extended cab. They sniffed around in tight circles and collapsed next to each other. They looked exhausted. Must have been a tiring night for them, all that roughhousing and all.

Once we were safely out of Dodge and on the New York State Thruway, Debbie started the conversation: "So, what else did you learn?"

"Catherine is living with a fellow named Cosmo in Camden. She was up here visiting, but we just missed her."

"How bad is it?"

"Very. She's an addict and a kept woman who does sexual acts for drugs."

"Oh God, that's awful." She hung her head in her hands.

"Yeah, but we can save her. We *will* save her."

"What if she doesn't want to be saved? I've reached out to her a few times, but she never answered."

"That was a while ago, right? Maybe she wasn't ready then. Maybe she is now. Either way, we can't *not* do this. No matter what, whether she wants us to or not, we *are* going to get her and bring her home."

Debbie reached over and traced her fingers over the back of my hand, then rested them on top of mine. "When I first met you, I knew you were something special."

I didn't say anything. I looked at her and smiled, bathing in the rare compliment she had given me.

We rolled into Eminence around noon, and even though we were starved, we decided to shower the Newburgh grime and nut-squeezer's blood off us before we ate lunch. We hadn't had a good meal in a while and was looking forward to it.

I let the dogs out into the backyard, and Buddy was in his glory with all the fresh new scents to tackle. The rabbits threw him for a loop though. He saw them, they froze, he approached them tentatively, with his nostrils twitching like mad, and when he came too close for comfort, they hopped away and disappeared under the shed. He followed them and sniffed around a little, then came steamrolling back to play with Saber.

Debbie and I watched them from the dining room table while we ate some lunch.

"We should give him a real name," She said. "You can't just keep calling him Buddy."

"I think the name fits. He's like Saber's best bud."

"You lack imagination."

"He followed me home, so I name him. Buddy it is."

We took a nap, and then it was time to get to work on this Cosmo fellow. Debbie ran some errands while I used TOR and HFS to find out all I could about him.

Holy crap, was it ugly.

His base of operations was in Camden, and he controlled all of Camden's north end, from I-676 and Route 30 on up to the Delaware River. While Newburgh certainly had its share of problems, Camden was in a league of its own. At one point last year, they were so broke they'd laid off fifty percent of their police force. The unemployment rate was almost twenty percent, and most of the jobs that were in Camden were low-paying. It always ranked near the top of the United States in murders, rapes, and other violent crimes. It was unbelievable that we had cities like this in such a great country.

Cosmo's biggest-earning heroin house, bringing in about $30K a week, was on Bailey Street, a one-way street so decrepit that almost every house was either abandoned or boarded up. He stationed a few men on the corner to steer addicts his way, and to warn of any cops that weren't on his payroll, of which there were few.

As good as Camden was to him and his cash hoard, he chose to live in Chairsville, a nearby suburb to the east, on a couple of acres of land with a well-manicured lawn. His two favorite nonsexual passions were hoarding cash and playing golf, both of which played a prominent role in his backyard. One buried underneath it, the other spread across it like a mini PGA course.

His entire kingdom was protected by an eight-foot-high black wrought-iron fence. His security was topped off by a driveway gate operated from either a keypad on one of the stone pillars that supported it, or from inside the house. It was an old standalone system, and since it wasn't connected to the outside world, there was no way to hack into it.

The entire property had high-tech security cameras that covered every inch of it. It was impossible to gain access to his house without being picked up by the security cameras, unless you hacked into the system. So I did.

Once inside, I got a feel for the house, a five-bedroom colonial with a full finished basement. He had the latest in electronics and furnishings, some over-the-top design pieces, and a room full of mounted animal heads with an occasional armless statue thrown in for poor taste.

After a few hours of studying the layout, I had everything figured out. Except the front gate. How was I going to rescue Catherine if I couldn't hack the front gate? Then it came to me...

19

AFTER A GREAT HOME-COOKED DINNER, Debbie sat on the couch next to me and took a sip of her wine. "So let's go over our plan."

I swirled my bourbon around the ice in my glass. "We head out tomorrow. Why don't we Barry White and chill tonight, and we can go over the plan in the morning?" Barry White was code for that whole Netflix and chill thing, which we took to a level that those Netflix aficionados could only dream about.

"No dice. I'll be thinking about it all night, and I won't be able to enjoy myself. You wouldn't want that, would you?"

I thought about it for a second, knowing full well that once I started pleasuring her, I could take her mind off a nuclear explosion in our backyard, but decided against pushing it. "Okay, fine. Here's the plan. I fly down to New

Jersey in my Cessna. I'll rent a van for you before I leave. You drive the van down and meet me at the airport. With the HFS intel, it was easy to hack into Cosmo's smart home, so I can program the AC unit to turn off and the heat to go on. They have a service contract with Axis Heating & Cooling, and after they fiddle with the thermostats and have no luck stopping the hot air, they'll call and schedule an emergency service call. I've tapped into the house phone, and after the AC starts blowing hot air, I'll redirect the house phone calls to a burner phone."

I stood up and retrieved an old-style flip phone from my go bag. "You'll answer on this and set up a service call. In the meantime, we'll break into the Axis parking lot and steal one of their vans. They have quite a few, and it'll be over the weekend, so no one will notice the missing van."

"Don't they get emergency calls over the weekend?"

"They won't have any this weekend. I'm taking down Axis's phone service, so all incoming phone calls will go direct to the voicemail system instead of rolling over to the answering service after three rings. They'll have quite a few angry messages come Monday morning, that's for sure. I'll set up an admin passcode in the voicemail system for us so we can check messages, just in case the clowns at Cosmo's house are too lazy to get up and use the house phone."

Debbie studied me and took another sip of wine. "I'm liking this. Go on."

"I'll grab a pair of overalls from the Axis office when we

get the keys to the van, and I'll pose as the repairman, which is how I'll gain access to the house."

"Okay, then what? Kill everybody and rescue Catherine? I love it!" She leaned over to high-five me.

I left her hanging. "Er, not so fast. I wish it was that easy, but they always have between six and ten men inside the house. They actually live there, along with Cosmo, Catherine, and a few other ladies. It's like a giant weaponized frat house."

"That's not good."

"No, and since I'm an outsider who can't be trusted, they'll all be on their toes. Watching me like a hawk. It'd be foolish for one guy to take on that many."

"Right. So..."

I went back to my go bag and took out a can of Freon. It was about the size of a one-liter soda bottle with a hose attached to it. A digital timer was duct-taped to its side. "This is sleeping gas. I'll connect it to the system and set the timer to disperse into the ductwork of the HVAC system at four a.m. Even if some of them are still awake, they won't smell anything. Ten minutes after the can's emptied, they should all be passed out. I'll walk right in and carry Catherine out."

Debbie frowned, and I could see that she'd already thought of the first problem. "But how will you know how much of this stuff to put in the house? What if you put in too much and kill everyone? Or not enough, and everyone is wide awake?"

"Right. I thought of that, so I worked the math out to be conservative. The medical term is twilight anesthesia. Once you know the square footage of the house and the subject's bodyweight, the calculation is quite simple. That assumes that there's no other source of ventilation, like an open window, which in this heat is very unlikely. Nobody should OD with my twilight calculations, but if one of the smaller occupants is really high, this could put them over the edge and possibly kill them. On the downside, the conservative twilight calculation won't knock everyone out."

"Well, that's no good. You could be back to being outnumbered."

"Honestly, that's likely to happen since I had to math out the dosage using Catherine's bodyweight. That means that the anesthetic will have less effect on the fatties and muscle heads, some of whom must be more than twice her weight. The good news is that I'll still have two things going for me. First, I'll surprise them. Second, the sleeping gas will help, even if they aren't knocked out. The ones who are drunk or stoned will likely be hardcore KO'd. The rest will at least be groggy and have delayed reflexes. Taking them out will be a walk in the park."

"Hmm. All right, it definitely has potential. I need to sleep on it to come up with worst-case scenario questions."

My eyes lit up. "Oh, I guess we're done? Does that mean it's Barry White time?"

She looked at me and smiled.

20

I USED one of my burner IDs and credit cards to rent a van that Debbie would be driving down to New Jersey, a five-hour ride. Our plan was to have her meet me at a small airstrip just outside of Camden. We'd stay in the van until the following day, which was a Saturday, when we would wreak our HVAC havoc.

After sending Debbie on her way, I loaded up my Cessna and confirmed the weather for my night flight. As luck would have it, the weather was forecast to be clear with a half moon most of the way, but starting to cloud up as I approached New Jersey. I'm instrument-rated, which means that I can safely fly in inclement weather, but I don't do it a lot, and a pilot gathers rust fast in the instrument-flying venue, so I made sure I went over everything a second and third time.

At one hundred and fifty knots, the trip would take a

little over an hour. The en route weather was a little better than forecast, with light winds and good visibility. Before I knew it, I was lining up for the runway at my destination airport.

I landed, taxied to a tie-down spot, and shut down my Cessna. Debbie pulled up a few minutes later, and we unloaded the tools and equipment that we'd need to achieve mission success. I didn't want to have Debbie riding around with all the weapons in the back of the van. If she ever got pulled over and the Statie decided to search her vehicle, she'd be late in meeting me. By a few decades.

We left the airport and pulled into the parking lot of a shopping center. I parked in the corner, broke out my laptop, and using HFS intel, I logged in to the Axis security system. I disabled the alarm, added an admin code for my personal use, and paused the recordings of the sixteen different cameras they had throughout the parking lot and inside by the reception area of the office.

I logged in to their phone system and changed the routing of the afterhours call forwarding so that any incoming phone calls would go straight to the operator's voicemail box. If Cosmo or one of his henchmen were too lazy to get off the couch and use the house phone to arrange the service call, I wanted to be able to retrieve their message and have Debbie call them right back, so I set up a passcode for myself to check voicemails. I closed up my laptop and smiled at Debbie.

"We're all set with Axis. Let's do this."

We left and made our way over to the Axis office building. I got us past the parking lot gate using the new code I'd programmed, and we drove over to the rear entrance. I punched in the six-digit code and pulled the door open. I went into the secretary's office and over to the metal box that held all the keys to the vans, pocketing key number 18. I entered the small locker room and jimmied the lockers until I found a set of overalls that didn't smell too bad and almost fit my six-foot-six muscular frame.

I went out the back door. Debbie had pulled our van out to the street and was waiting with the headlights off.

I peeled off the magnetic AXIS signs on van 18, unlocked the driver's-side door, and climbed in. She started up on the first try, and I drove away.

Debbie followed me to a quiet little state park just outside of Medford, and we pulled into our side-by-side reserved camping spots. I climbed into her van and gave her a big kiss on the lips. Just another happy couple on a weekend getaway.

After a short nap, we unpacked and set up our equipment, which consisted of two MacBook Pros, complete with TOR browser of course, and two satellite links through HFS. We also had a spare Sierra Wireless Raven device, which was basically a cellular Wi-Fi hotspot, for backup.

At seven a.m. sharp, I ran Operation Hot Stuff and brought up Cosmo's thermostat on my laptop. We sat in the back of the van and watched as the temperature inside the house started climbing. Eighteen minutes after the temperature inside the house hit eighty-seven degrees, the burner cell phone rang.

21

DEBBIE ANSWERED the phone on the third ring. "Hello, Axis Heating and Cooling answering service. How may I help you?"

"Yeah, we got an emergency."

"Can you explain the nature of your emergency, sir?"

"Yeah, AC don't work. It's blowing hot air."

"Oh no. Can I have your name and address? I'll look up your account."

Debbie took down the info and pounded some keys on her laptop to give the impression of typing. "Hmm, I can't seem to find you here...oh, wait, there you are, sorry about that. Stupid computer. Let's see, soonest that I can get a technician out to your house is today after lunch. Will someone be there between noon and six p.m.?"

"Yeah. But can't you get someone here sooner? Hot as shit in here."

"Oh, I'm sorry, sir, but being a weekend and all..."

"Yeah. Someone will be here. Just have him hit the buzzer at the front gate when he gets here."

"I'll tell the technician that. Thank you for your business, and you have a nice day, sir." Debbie flipped the phone closed and smiled at me. "Okay, you're in, Mr. HVAC technician. That was almost *too* easy."

"Don't jinx me."

She smacked me on the forehead. "Listen, Patrick, there's no such thing as a 'jinx.' You make this work."

"Of course I will. Now, let's go launch Amelia and get a good look at Cosmo's crib."

I let Debbie drive while I programmed the HFS drone software. Amelia would have to fly higher than normal over the residence, since I couldn't take a chance on anyone hearing her. Cosmo's house was located in a quiet area, and even a drone as small as Amelia could be heard from a few hundred feet away. As far as the FAA was concerned, I couldn't legally fly a drone higher than four hundred feet, but since this was life-critical, I decided to break that law.

We found a small playground that had a kids' swing set and some monkey bars. We pulled into the empty parking lot, and when I finished programming Amelia, I launched her from the back of the van.

She went straight up in the air, hovered for a second at five hundred feet, and made a beeline for Cosmo's. I watched the live feed on my iPhone as she got closer to the front of his house and started her orbit. She got about halfway around when I spotted two shirtless men with muscles out the wazoo, in the backyard with three topless white women. They were drinking Molsons and sunning themselves by the in-ground pool. I eyed them closely to see if one of the women was Catherine.

A blonde woman with a cupid tattoo on her left breast shielded her eyes and pointed in the air. I was caught up in using my zoom lens to study the intricacies of her beautiful artwork, and it took a second, or three, for it to register that she was pointing at Amelia. So much for my stealthiness. Or focus.

One of the men reached under his lounge chair and pulled out a Mossberg 500 shotgun with a pistol grip. Before I could react, he fired two blasts at Amelia. He missed, and I hit the auto-land button. My mighty drone tore ass out of there at her max speed of a whopping twenty-eight miles per hour. Two minutes later she landed next to the rear of the van.

"Wow, that was quick," Debbie commented. "Almost as fast as you the other night."

I scooped up Amelia and jumped into the back of the van, slamming the doors behind me. "Drive. Now."

She must have sensed the urgency in my voice, because she gunned the van and we took off out of the parking lot and down the street. I watched out the rear window with my hand on my Glock just in case we were being followed. I didn't see anyone.

A few seconds later, I heard the loud rumble of motorcycles coming from the other direction. I turned and looked through the front windshield. Two shirtless muscles-out-the-wazoo men on Harleys thundered by us and turned into the parking lot of the playground.

Debbie made a right at the first intersection, and as we turned the corner, I saw the two Harleys leave the playground parking lot and head in our direction.

Uh-oh...

22

LEO KENNEDY WENT over to his supervisor's office and was waved in before he had a chance to knock.

"Come in, Leo. I need you to drop what you're doing and head on over to Newburgh. The shit's hit the fan. Must have been a full moon. Two local cops stumbled upon a drug deal gone bad and recovered two thousand in cash and about two million dollars' worth of heroin."

"That's a great haul. But—wait a minute... only two thousand in cash? That's an eyebrow raiser. You'd expect a lot more cash with that quantity of heroin."

"Yes, but that's not why you're going in. We can look at the prospect of missing cash at a later date. There was a full-blown shoot-out at a heroin house on Landers Street. So far, we have seven deceased. All males. Plus we have three females in the hospital."

"They expected to survive?"

"Fortunately, yes. Believe it or not, two of the females are in the hospital to have duct tape surgically removed from their eyes."

"What? Who duct-tapes eyes? That's sick!"

"Crazy, right? First time I've seen that in my life. It could've been much worse for them, though. They were in the heroin house when the gunmen showed up and started shooting."

"They give descriptions?"

"Yes, but they only saw one perp. Tall, Caucasian. Called themselves the Old Fuckin' White Guys."

"You're joking."

"I wish I were, but they both swore it. The cops interviewed them separately, and their stories matched to a T. Vasquez is out sick, so I want you to grab Russel Blake and do some digging."

"Sure. But why are we getting involved? Shouldn't this be a local police problem?"

"Ordinarily, yes. But our president is all gung ho about gang arrests, and this has to be gang-related."

"Maybe it was a straight-up robbery?"

"No, too many things in motion. A family on a fishing boat was awakened close to dawn by someone drowning in the Hudson. They managed to get a spotlight on him, but he disappeared before they could rescue him."

"Could just be a coincidence..."

"Unlikely. They found the body washed up a few hours later. I just spoke to the medical examiner. The deceased had his eyelids ripped off. And there appears to be some type of residue on his face. As in duct tape residue. The Newburgh cops ID'd the guy as a local dealer."

"Could be the work of a serial killer. Or maybe a vigilante?"

"I want you to put the Lamburt thing on hold. No way he's involved in all of this. Interview the female witnesses at the hospital. See if you can get a better description of the shooter. After you've finished with them, check in with me, and by then I'll have more for you. Dismissed."

"Roger. Will do, sir." Leo went back to his desk, gathered all his notes on Lamburt, and stuffed them in a folder. He opened a drawer and tossed them inside. Cefalo must be right. There was no way one man could inflict that much destruction...

23

DEBBIE STAYED CALM. She made two quick rights and lost the steroid junkies without breaking a sweat. She was much better at this sort of thing than I gave her credit for.

"Good work. You lost them."

She nodded. "Get any good footage?"

"I don't know. Let's circumvent the area and take the long way back to the campsite. Then we can check the video." I felt the van turn before I finished my sentence.

"Already on it," she said.

With all the running in circles we did, it took us nearly an hour to get back to the campsite, but at least I was sure we weren't tailed. While Debbie was making us hard to follow, I downloaded Amelia's video to my laptop. We pulled into our spot and I hit play. The video was short, only a few minutes long, and aside from the closeup of the topless woman, it didn't have much to offer. Debbie didn't appreciate that.

"Jeez, Jack, you're like a teenage boy. You see a nice pair of tits and your brain gets hijacked. You could have at least filmed the information you were looking for before you zoomed in on her tits."

"What? I was calibrating the lens."

She didn't buy it. "You're a terrible liar, Patrick. Now you're stuck with intel from Google Earth and HFS."

"Don't worry, I already have a backup plan. I'll see enough of the backyard to confirm what I need to. I'll make this work."

"You better. It's not just the rescue that's at stake with this part of the op. Our lives are, and there's no room for error."

I ate my granola bar lunch and washed it down with a protein shake. I checked my watch. It was go time, so I left our van, stuck the magnetic signs back on the Axis van, and kissed Debbie goodbye. "I should be back within two to three hours. If anything goes wrong, go back to Eminence and wait for me there. I don't want you anywhere near this place if the shit hits the fan." I hopped in the van and headed over to Cosmo's house.

Twenty minutes later, I pulled up to the front gate at his house, rolled down my window, and pressed the intercom button. I was met with the same grouchy voice that had called Debbie on the phone earlier.

"Yeah?"

I used the name on my uniform. Not sure if I pronounced it correctly, but so what? "Barry Eisler, Axis Heating and Cooling, here for your service call."

"Yeah, 'bout time. Hot as shit in here."

What a dick. The big iron gate swung open, and I pulled up the curved driveway. I made a mental note that when all this was done, I would set up the HVAC software to turn their heat on every morning. I could hack into their water meter and turn that off too, maybe kill any who survived tonight by dehydration...

I watched through my side-view mirror as the gate thunked to a close. I was officially inside the lion's den, with no way out unless they let me.

I parked the van by the front of the house, grabbed my toolbox from the back, and hopped up the wide steps to a massive oak front door. Before I could finger the bell, a swarthy-looking middle-aged man swung open the door. The heat from the house poured out and carried with it body odor that would have made me gag if I wasn't busy fighting back the urge to smile.

He was short and built like a fridge, typical Jersey boy. Must be something in the drinking water. He had on denim shorts that hung down past his knees and a loose-fitting T-shirt, and he was carrying a red bandanna that he wiped his brow with.

"Afternoon," I said. "I understand you have a problem with your HVAC?"

He looked up at me and his eyes widened. "Holy shit, big mutha, ain't you?"

I smiled down at him. "Your HVAC? You have a problem?"

"Yeah, you're damn right we do. Bitch is blowing hot air." Grouchy sighed and wiped the back of his neck with his bandanna.

"All right, the first thing I need to do is check your thermostat. Can you show me where it is?"

He nodded and waved me in. "Take your shoes off."

He closed the door behind me, and I left my shoes on a tray next to an umbrella stand. There were five other pairs of shoes there, mostly Nike sneakers. Mine were the biggest, by far.

He led me to the family room. It had movie-theater style seating, two rows of four, and a huge TV on the wall. ESPN was talking about baseball, and a couple of wide guys sat on the couch drinking beer and eating chips. They never took their eyes off me. I nodded to them, and one of them grunted, "What's up."

There was a young lady sprawled out on a futon, glued to her smartphone. It was Catherine! Holy crap, she looked just like a tired, thinner version of Debbie. With bigger tits. Wow, much bigger tits... My mind raced back to the photo I'd seen on Jorge's phone.

She looked up at me. I smiled and nodded.

She ignored me and went back to her smartphone.

Grouchy pointed to the thermostat. "There it is. You

need a freaking college degree to figure that thing out."

Right.

I pretended to manipulate it while I looked around to get a feel for the place. Seeing it live was much better then looking through hacked security cams, and after a few minutes, I had all the intel I needed. I turned to look down at Grouchy, who was standing behind me and watching me like a hawk. "Well, I think it's a compressor issue."

"What's that?"

"That big unit with a fan that sits just outside the house, usually on the side of the house."

"I have no idea where it is."

"That's okay, I'll walk around the outside of the house and find it." I bent down and picked up my toolbox. I went over to the front door, slid into my shoes, and opened the door. I turned to Grouchy to let him know that I'd knock on the door when I was done, and he was right in my chest.

"Yeah, I need to go with you." He wiped his upper lip with the bandanna and yelled over his shoulder to one of his buddies on the couch. "Yo, Keith, I'm outside with the air conditioner guy."

I stepped outside, trying to figure out a way to lose my tail. I didn't mind being followed around outside, but I needed a few minutes alone in the basement. If I couldn't get rid of him, I wouldn't be able to set up the sleeping gas canister in the air supply duct, and my whole plan would be shot to hell.

Then, it came to me...

24

I LED him around to the right side of the house, where the driveway led to a three-car garage. I knew that the compressor wasn't on that side, but I needed to get a good look at the backyard. My little peeping Tom adventure with Amelia only captured part of it, and I needed to verify a few things before I could proceed with the rescue.

We turned the corner, and the whole yard opened up. I saw the patio that the cupid-tattooed blonde had been sunbathing on with her friends, but they were nowhere to be found now. The two Harley riders were there though. They were over by a shed near the side of the property, fueling up their roadsters. They looked our way and nodded when they saw Grouchy leading me across the yard.

The three-hole golf course was a short par three, and right away I saw a problem that hadn't shown up on my Google Earth research. A potential deal killer.

There was a tree right in the middle of the yard.

I filed that important tidbit away and proceeded to scope out the rest of the yard. The trees surrounding the property line were mostly evergreens. For privacy, no doubt. So that worked out well, because the tallest one was only about twenty feet high. The golf course itself had a few sand traps but it wasn't very hilly, so that was a big bonus.

I found the compressor unit by the side of the house and pretended to run some test on it. Grouchy watched me, but I could tell by the way his eyes glazed over when I explained things to him that he was bored as hell and not paying attention.

After twenty minutes, I put all the components together with a deep sigh. "Well, the good news is the everything seems to be working okay. The bad news is that it must be a bad evaporator coil, and if it is, I'm not sure if I have one in the van."

Grouch perked up. "Evapa-what? And what happens if you don't have one in the van?"

"Evaporator coil. It sits on top of the furnace and cools the air before it reaches the rooms. If I don't have one, then maybe I can do a Band-Aid fix, just enough to get you guys some cool air until the part comes in. Let's head to the furnace and take a look-see."

He led me around to the front of the house and over to the front door, instructed me to take my shoes off, and led me into the basement. We passed by the family room on the way, and I saw Catherine again. I felt excited seeing her in person. I'd heard so much about her and learned so much from my HFS research that I felt like I knew her already. She ignored me.

We reached the bottom of the basement stairs, and Grouchy led me to the left and into a utility room, where the furnace sat. I took out some tools and started working on opening the ductwork access panel to get to the evaporator coil.

Everything about my plan—the success or failure of the entire mission—hinged on the next few minutes. I tried to remain calm and sound natural. "Where's the circuit breaker for the furnace?"

"What?" Grouchy looked up at me with a moist, furrowed forehead.

"The circuit breaker. There's a main electrical panel box somewhere in the house that has shutoffs to the different end points of electricity. One for the stove, one for the HVAC, the kitchen outlets, etc., etc."

"I have no idea."

I finished removing the access panel to the air duct supply that housed the evaporator coil and put it on the floor. I took out my flashlight and lit up the inside of the duct, pretending to examine the coil. I hmmm'ed a few times and put my tools down. "I can't do any more work without turning the breaker off. I'll go look for it." I went to leave the room.

He put his arm straight out on front of me and I stopped and looked at him.

He had an even more serious face on. "No. I'll go find it. You stay here. Don't leave this room."

Yes!

I put on my best "shocked" look and raised my hands in surrender. "Okay, okay, fine. No need to get upset." I turned away and pretended to work on the furnace, a big lotto-winning smile painted across my face.

He left the room and closed the door, giving me extra privacy. I went into my tool bag and dug out the Freon canister and some duct tape. God, I loved that stuff. I might have to join Duct Tape Users Anonymous after this mission.

I double-checked the correct timing on the digital timer and taped the canister inside and against the far corner of the air supply duct. I pressed the start button and watched the countdown proceed. Perfect.

I opened the HFS app on the iPhone and killed the software program that was wreaking havoc on the thermostat. I put my phone away and started to put back the access panel.

I heard the door push open and Grouchy came back in: "Yeah, I couldn't find it."

I turned and looked at him like an excited little kid. "We don't need it. I fixed it! It was a loose wire to the evaporator coil. I'll be out of your hair in five minutes." I finished tightening up the fasteners, threw my tools in my bag, and smiled at him. "All done!"

He led me up the stairs, and I took one more look at Catherine as I passed the family room. She was still sitting on the futon and playing with her phone. She looked up at me, and I could swear she flashed a quick smile. But I think that about every woman I make eye contact with, so maybe not.

I put my shoes on and left the building.

I threw my tools in the van, got in, and drove away. As soon as I was clear of the front gate, I called Debbie. She answered on the first ring. "How'd it go?"

"Done. And I saw your sister."

"How'd she look?"

"Tired, but other than that she looked all right. I recognized her right away. Same eyes as you."

"You bringing the van back to Axis now? Want me to meet you there?"

"No, not until tonight. I'll see you in a few." I pulled over on a quiet street, removed the magnetic signs and tossed them in the back. I was back at the campground in ten minutes, and Debbie was waiting outside the van with a big smile on her beautiful face.

We spent the rest of the day lounging around and taking naps inside the rental van. I was getting antsy and felt like doing something, so we returned the Axis van to its rightful spot. Everything was working out perfect, and I didn't want to take a chance on breaking into the office building to return the keys and coveralls, so I left the keys on the front seat and threw the stinky coveralls in a dumpster.

We returned to the campground around nine and had a light meal of a vanilla protein shake and a granola bar. With nothing to do but wait, we continued our lounge fest until a little after eleven, when we fell asleep.

I woke up before the alarm and looked at my phone. Ten to three. I lay there thinking about my plan, going over it again and again, looking for the tiniest of flaws that could compromise the mission, but I couldn't find any. I knew that this was going to work out perfectly.

Boy, was I in for a rude awakening...

25

WE LEFT the campground at 4:15 sharp, and while Debbie drove us to the airstrip, I opened my laptop and logged in to Cosmo's security system.

The first cams I clicked on were in the family room with the two rows of theater seats and the massive TV. It was dark, the only light coming from the TV, and the security cams had a tough time adjusting to the rapidly changing lighting from the TV show, so it wasn't the best image. I did see at least four people in the seats, all men, but there could have been more. None of them moved, which was a good sign, but I couldn't tell for sure if they were asleep or just vegging.

I looked at the kitchen cams, and there was no one there. No one in the hallway either. Or the basement. All was quiet on every cam in the house, a great sign.

"Looking good, babe. We're a go for launch."

Debbie pulled into the little airstrip and dropped me off at my plane. We transferred all our tools to my airplane, and she drove the van into a corner of the field and killed the engine. She grabbed my sanitizer-soaked wipes, gave the interior a good cleaning to remove all of our DNA, and threw the wipes in a Ziploc bag before jogging back to my plane.

My Cessna 206 has six seats and weighs in fully loaded at thirty-six hundred pounds, twelve hundred of which can be the useful load, which is fancy pilot speak for people, fuel, and cargo. Since this mission required a short takeoff and landing, I removed everything that wasn't essential to flight, including excess fuel and the four passenger seats.

When I'd first acquired my plane, I'd made modifications to help with short takeoff and landings, or STOLs. Vortex generators and wingtip extensions along with a light gross weight of just under three thousand pounds lowered the takeoff and landing speeds to what felt like a fast jog, but it could be tricky staying safe at such a low airspeed, especially if there were wind gusts involved.

The biggest hurdle with this mission was that I had to land power off. Short landings are much easier with power on because I can use the throttle to fine-tune my touchdown adjustments and the plane can fly slower with the prop forcing wind over the wings. I had no choice but to make a power-off approach to Cosmo's backyard because otherwise the aircraft engine noise would alert the neighbors. I had to kill the engine at altitude and glide in, which meant that once I started my approach, I was committed to finishing it. Which meant that I was going to land in that backyard, on Cosmo's little three-hole golf course, even if a herd of Buffalo came thundering through right before touchdown.

Debbie stood by while I preflighted the aircraft, and I could tell she was nervous because she never stopped pacing the entire time. Funny how someone who'd been through what she had in the military could be nervous about anything. I guess it's hard giving up control and surrendering your destiny to another.

I finished and held out my hand to help her in the plane. "Your chariot awaits you, my dear."

"Never mind chariot. Just get your game face on and do your job."

I closed the door after she got in and checked one more time that the three tie-down lines were no longer connected. I climbed into the left seat, yelled, "Clear," and turned the key. The three-hundred-horsepower Lycoming engine started right away, with a deep throaty rumble that made the plane tremble and my testosterone level surge.

I gave Debbie her headset and put mine on, adjusted the squelch and volume, and did a headset check. "How do you hear me?"

"Fine."

"You're loud and clear too," I said.

"Roger."

I taxied over to the end of the grass runway, lined up for

takeoff, and pushed the throttle all the way in. I estimated that we weighed in at a scrawny 2,870 pounds, and with all the STOL modifications and some excellent pilot technique, we were off the ground in a couple of hundred feet. I stayed close to the ground, in what's called ground effect, until I reached seventy knots. I eased the yoke back, we started climbing, and I leveled off at one thousand feet.

I punched in the waypoint of Cosmo's house into my GPS even though it was only eleven miles from the airstrip. The night was calm and mostly clear except for a few clouds that played hide-and-seek with the half moon. I dimmed the interior lights to a minimum to help keep my night vision sharp.

My flight plan was to approach the house from the west, fly about a half mile south of the GPS waypoint so that I could see the house out the left side, like a normal landing is flown, and do a lights-out engine-out approach on the backyard golf course. That way none of the early-morning risers would see or hear me arrive, the only sound being the whisk of wind over the wings followed by a soft touchdown on the well-manicured golf course.

I thought about that small tree that had sprung up since the Google Earth imagery had been captured, but I should have enough wingspan clearance to land between it and the sand trap that was next to the eight-foot-high wrought-iron fence.

If not, we were dead.

I throttled back to a quiet fifteen hundred rpm, and we

slowed down to ninety knots. I flew to the waypoint on my GPS and passed about a half mile south of it, but I couldn't find the house.

Debbie broke the silence: "You see it anywhere?"

"No, but I know it's right there." I frowned and nodded toward the house. This was not good. I'd only allotted enough fuel for fifteen minutes for this leg of the flight. Any longer and we'd be dipping into the reserves as we got closer to my private airstrip in Eminence, which might force me to land somewhere to refuel. That was the last thing I wanted to do.

I initiated a slow left turn, keeping the GPS waypoint just off my left wingtip, and after a few more frantic seconds passed, I recognized the moonlit house. "Found it!"

Now all I had to do was land, clear the tree and sand trap, and not run long and into the wrought-iron fence at the end of the third green.

I got us positioned for the approach, never taking my eyes off my touchdown spot in the backyard. When the time was right, I cut the engine and all went silent except for the wind hitting the windshield. I put in ten degrees of flaps and waited for the aircraft to settle into her descent.

"Oh God," Debbie murmured through her headset.

"We don't need these anymore." I took mine off and tossed it in the back. Debbie did the same.

"This is freakin' me out, Jack."

"I need to focus. Tighten your seat belt. Sterile cockpit procedure from here to touchdown."

"What's that?"

"No more talking!"

My landing point in the dark backyard appeared in my windshield in the perfect spot, held steady for a few seconds, and started to drift lower. I was too high. I put in more flaps to add drag to the airframe and steepen our descent without gaining airspeed. The landing spot started to rise in the windshield. I was getting low, so I took out some flaps. We danced like this all the way to touchdown, a hard teeth-rattling jolt of an affair that made me smile. I retracted the flaps all the way and jammed on the brakes.

We skidded across the well-manicured lawn and hurtled toward the end of the golf course, where the wrought-iron fence was waiting to stop us if I couldn't.

"Fence!" Debbie yelled, just in case I didn't see it for myself. She leaned back in her seat, as if she could create distance between herself and the dashboard to minimize impact.

I pumped the brakes, trying to break the skid, but the turf wouldn't cooperate and we just kept sliding and tearing up the grass.

It didn't take much of a blow to knock an airplane prop out of balance, and if we hit that fence, even just a light bump, we'd be in big trouble. An unbalanced prop would vibrate so violently that it would shake the engine right off the plane. There was no way I could take off with a damaged prop and risk all our lives.

I jammed my feet on the brakes, and just when I was

sure that we were going to hit the fence, I felt the plane bog down and stop. We hit a sand trap.

Debbie didn't appreciate my piloting expertise as much as I did, and let me know about it as she undid her seat belt. "Never mind Patrick, I'm calling you Launchpad McQuack from now on." A reference to the goofy *DuckTales* pilot who always crashed at least five times per episode. I ignored her, but I could tell by the tone of her voice that she was relieved to be safe on the ground.

Even if we had just entered the lion's den...

26

I OPENED the cockpit door and stepped out onto the sand. I looked back at the mess I'd made of Cosmo's golf course and chuckled. I pictured the look on his face when he woke up in the morning, made his cup of coffee, and looked out the window in his kitchen to admire his well-manicured greens.

"Let's turn the plane around so she's ready to go, then I'm going in." We went to the tail, leaned on the elevator to take the weight off the nose wheel, and walked the tail around so the plane was pointed the right way for a quick getaway. It was a struggle moving in the sand, but between the two of us, we managed to get her turned in the right direction. We couldn't move her out of the sand, but I felt that the prop would handle that okay once I started her back up.

I grabbed my backpack that held my tools and weapons and gave Debbie a kiss. "I'm off."

I went up to a basement window and knelt down. I took out my Scorkl, a small portable breathing device with a tank that would give me ten minutes of fresh air. If I stayed in the house longer than that, I'd have to breath in the sleeping gas. I'd hate to pass out on the floor and wake up to Cosmo and his henchmen smiling down at me.

I attached a suction cup in the center of the window, and with my free hand, I used my glass cutter and etched a hole around it. With an audible crack, I removed the piece of glass and laid it on the mulch by my knees. I inserted my arm in the hole and unlocked the window. I opened it, slid through feet first, and ended up in the dark basement. I took the night vision goggles out of my backpack and put them on. I grabbed my Glock and screwed on my silencer.

I was in some sort of rec room. It was empty and smelled like Doritos and spilled beer. It had a single couch in front of a gigantic TV. It looked like an eighty-incher.

I found the stairs and took my time going up, trying to keep the squeaks down, which was no easy task for a big man like me. At the top of the stairs, I encountered a locked door. I picked the lock and swung the door open.

I recognized the family room straight in front of me. There were four people in the theater seats, and I couldn't tell if they were sleeping or knocked out. I had no time for frivolities, so I dismissed the urge to shoot them. I headed to the kitchen instead.

It was empty.

I went to the giant staircase that led to the second floor and started up. I didn't hear anything at all to indicate that anyone was awake, but I still took my time and went slow to make as little noise as possible.

I reached the top of the stairs, which led to a hallway with five doors. All were closed.

I tried the first one on the right. It was unlocked, and I opened it and stepped inside. A small bed was against the far wall, and it held two people. Both were naked. I recognized one as the muscles-out-the-wazoo guy who'd shot at Amelia. Lying next to him was a girl, maybe fifteen tops. She looked so young and innocent.

Muscles started to turn toward me, and he opened his eyes. He looked right at me but didn't move. His forehead furrowed, and I could see his Neanderthal mind trying to grasp what he was seeing. I pressed the gun against his forehead, covered it with a pillow, and pulled the trigger once for Amelia. He twitched a few times and was still. Between the silencer and pillow, I hardly heard anything.

Sixteen bullets left.

The girl was still out cold, so I let her be. I looked under the bed and checked the closet, just to be sure that I didn't miss a hiding person, and then let myself out, locking the door behind me.

I went down the hallway to the second door and found it locked. I saved that one for later.

The third door was unlocked, and I swung it inwards and stepped into the room. Empty.

The fourth door was unlocked. I stepped in, and there was Catherine, sleeping like a baby in a king-sized bed. Naked. Of course she was. Spitting image of Debbie, except she was skinnier with less muscle tone, and her breasts were twice as large. No way those things were real.

I wrapped her in a sheet and picked her up with both arms. I carried her to the door, peeked out into the hallway to make sure that it was empty, and hustled down the stairs. Between my breathing device, my night vision goggles, and her skin sliding against the satin sheets that I'd wrapped her in, it was awkward carrying her. Plus her fake breasts must have added an extra ten pounds, so I had to take it slow.

My breathing increased in the excitement of almost being out of the house—it had nothing to do with carrying a naked woman in my arms—and my breather tube went dry.

I couldn't just spit it out and leave it there, because my DNA was all over it, so I had to drop it in Catherine's lap and make sure I held her nice and tight against me so that the breather tube didn't slide down between us and fall to the floor.

I managed to get to the front door without dropping my Glock, the breather tube, or Catherine, when the lights went on...

27

FBI AGENT LEO KENNEDY answered his cell phone on the third ring. "Kennedy."

"Leo, it's Paul. You got a minute?"

"Sure."

"Where are you?"

"Blake and I just finished interviewing the two young ladies at the hospital. We arrived just in time. They were about to be released, none the worse for wear after their eye-taping episode."

"Okay, good. A few minutes ago the Newburgh police chief called. They dragged the Hudson and found two fifty-gallon drums sitting at the bottom of it. They each contained a body. The drums are still on their boat, so we don't know too much, except that the deceased appear to have been shot with a high-powered weapon. Forensics is on the boat now. Can you and Blake swing by the docks and take a look?"

"Yes, sir. We can be there in twenty minutes."

"Very good. You get any pertinent info out of your hospital interviews?"

"I'm not sure, sir. We're dealing with addicts, so their statements have to be rated as unreliable."

"Noted. What'd they say?"

"Stand by, sir." Leo took the phone from his ear and placed it on speaker. "Can you hear me okay, sir?"

"Yeah, you're fine."

"Give me a second, sir." Leo tapped his Evernote app and scrolled down to the witness statements. "Okay, here we go, sir. And I quote— 'Spoke nice. Good English. Tall, white, handsome, muscular.'" Leo paused for a second. "And they were in agreement on this next line, sir." He cleared his throat. "'Big bulge in pants. He was totally doable.'"

"Seriously?"

"Swear to God."

"That's going to look great on the wanted posters."

28

I KNEW what had happened as soon as the first explosion of light hammered my eyes. I slammed them shut, dropped Catherine on the floor with a thud, and ripped off my night vision goggles. I rolled forward and came up pointing my Glock.

Grouchy was standing in the kitchen, holding a shotgun and looking a little drunk and a lotta confused. He slurred his words and was unsteady on his feet, weaving from side to side. He looked up at me, blinked a few times, and tried to shake the cobwebs from his head.

"Air conditioner guy?"

"That's right, and I didn't take my shoes off either."

I shot him twice in the chest.

Fourteen bullets left.

He stumbled backwards and fell down the five steps to the family room, smacking down flat on his back. When he hit, he squeezed off a shotgun blast, tearing the weapon out of his death grip and sending it spinning across the floor. Anybody within ten miles who was asleep, drug-induced or not, was awake. Including Catherine.

Every light in the house came on. Some outside too. A loud siren went off, one of those piercing home security kinds, and I was sure that the cops were being autodialed.

Two men came crawling up from the family room, and I shot them both in the chest. They stumbled backwards and landed on Grouchy.

I went to help Catherine up, and she punched me in the face, kicked me in the nuts, and grabbed a vase from the front door entry table and smashed it over my head. Good thing it was one of those fragile two-thousand-year-old Chinese types. It shattered into a hundred pieces and I didn't feel a thing.

My nuts were killing me, though. Man, they had taken a beating the last few days.

Catherine turned to run and I grabbed her from behind and rear naked choked her unconscious. I threw her over my shoulder, found my breather bottle, opened the front door and tore ass down the steps. I ran around the garage side of the house and into the backyard.

I heard the back door slide open, and two men with pistols came staggering out onto the patio. I saw the suppressed flash of the Remington explode twice and knew I didn't have to worry about them.

Debbie opened the cargo door, and together we placed

Catherine inside the airplane. "Jesus, Jack, she's naked. Couldn't you at least cover her up? My God. Her tits are huge."

"I did, and I noticed. Now climb in and hold her tight during takeoff. Might be bumpy."

Debbie jumped in, and I closed and locked the cargo door behind her. I ran around to the left cockpit door and climbed in. I turned the key and pumped the throttle once, and the mighty Lycoming engine roared alive. Flaps ten degrees, brakes on, full power, and release brakes.

We didn't go anywhere. Still bogged down in the sand.

I pulled the yoke all the way back, and the airflow from the prop blast forced the tail of the airplane down just enough to raise the nose wheel out of the sand. Now that the nose wheel was free, we started to roll. Agonizingly slow at first, but once we cleared the sand, we really started moving, and it wasn't long before we were bouncing across the lawn like a runaway Tonka tank.

I kept the control yoke full back to keep as much weight off the nose wheel as possible, and about halfway across the yard, I felt the big Cessna struggle to get airborne and waddle into the air. I lowered the nose to stay in ground effect and build up airspeed.

Ground effect was a physics phenomenon where an airplane could lift off the ground at a lower airspeed than it could actually fly. The wings compressed the air against the earth's surface and added extra lift, similar to when a bird swoops down and glides across the top of the ocean for a long time before having to flaps its wings to stay airborne.

Alaskan bush pilots had perfected this technique decades ago, taking off from a rough or muddy surface. They'd lift off as slow as possible, lower the nose to stay just a few feet above the ground, and without the drag of the landing gear on the rough surface they'd build up speed faster and be able to gain altitude sooner. Once the airplane is more than a wingspan's width above the ground, all benefits of ground effect go the way of the dodo bird, and the normal rules of flight apply.

But I needed altitude. Right now. The wrought-iron fence grew bigger and bigger in my windshield, and if we didn't clear that, we'd all die. It didn't matter if we only crashed from eight feet high. Other then a seat belt, small general aviation airplanes have zilch in the way of crash survival built into them. Everything in aviation is engineered to keep the aircraft light, and crash testing is not part of the certification process.

At the last second before impact, I yanked hard on the yoke and we cleared the fence.

"Holy crap, that was close," Debbie yelled up to me.

The stall warning horn blared, indicating that if we went any slower we'd lose aerodynamic lift, and like a water skier that was going too slow, we'd sink. Except that this wouldn't be a slow or soft sink. We'd end up leaving what Chuck Yeager called "a smoking hole."

I dropped the nose to gain some airspeed, and we flew

through the neighbor's yard so low that we triggered their motion detectors and the backyard lights came on. I wondered if they had a security camera, and if it started recording automatically when the lights came on. Good thing I'd thought ahead and covered the ID numbers painted on the sides of my airplane, because if this hit YouTube, we'd break the internet faster than a naked Kardashian's butt shelving a glass of champagne.

We skimmed the water in the neighbor's above-ground pool and my right wingtip took out his folded-up pool ladder with a clang that reminded me of a home run I'd hit in Little League with an aluminum bat.

We were still flying though, and I steered the Cessna between two trees and into the next neighbor's yard, still unable to climb out of ground effect. Every time I started to gain some airspeed, I hit something that slowed me down.

Thank God the neighbor didn't have any pool ladders, but he did have one of those inflatable kids' fun houses set up in the middle of his yard.

I quick glanced at my airspeed indicator, and just as I thought, I still didn't have enough airspeed to climb out of ground effect, although I managed to steer us around the pink fun house.

Most of it, anyway. I sliced through the corner of it with about two feet of my right wing. In my peripheral vision, and with the help of their motion-detector-triggered security lighting, I saw the whole pink house, complete with a gigantic birthday cake painted on it, lift off the ground. We carried it for a few seconds, the nose of the airplane yawing hard to the right from the added drag of the rapidly deflating fun house, before it slipped off my wingtip and fluttered down into their neighbor's yard.

I prayed that none of the birthday party kids were camping out in it...

Without hitting any more objects, my powerful little airplane was able to gain some speed, and a few seconds after my playhouse home-wrecking affair, my airspeed indicator passed through seventy, and I slid the yoke back and we started our climb. We cleared the adjoining neighbor's tree line with a few feet to spare and were on our way.

I turned and looked at Debbie and Catherine. They were sitting up in the cargo area and hugging each other so tight I thought they would cut off each other's circulation. Catherine was crying into her sister's shoulder, and even with only the soft glow of the instrument panel, I could see that they were ghostly white.

I handed Debbie her headset and she put it on.

"How do you read me?"

"That was awful, Jack."

"How's she holding up?"

"Terrible. Could you have made the takeoff any more harrowing? I think I soiled my pants. Not funny."

"Sorry. But we made it."

"Just get us home safe." She took the headset off and threw it at me, nailing me in the back of the head. I guess our conversation was over. Sheesh, women. I'd just displayed the greatest skill in piloting since Sully landed in the Hudson, and she wasn't happy.

I focused on the flying, enjoying the slow rise of the sun over the mountains to the east, and in less than an hour I was making a more traditional power-on landing at my grass strip in Eminence. Sure did feel good to be home. I pulled up to my hangar and shut down the engine.

Saber and Buddy came tearing out of the doggie door to see what all the commotion was. Despite his stoic appearance, Saber was always glad to greet us with a wagging stub of a tail. Buddy, on the other hand, didn't have any appearance other than a rambunctious fun-loving puppy attitude that, no matter what your mood, made you smile.

I ran into the house and grabbed a robe for Catherine. She put it on and looked at me with a scowl like I was Hitler reincarnated. She started to sob and clung tight to Debbie. Saber walked over and put a paw across her lap, then laid his head on it.

Debbie looked at me with a furrowed forehead. "What happened back there?"

"It kind of went downhill fast. There was a lot of close-up violence and a high body count. I'm sure she feared for her life, probably thought I was a hired killer. I bet that's why she's so upset."

"Or she could just be reliving your last takeoff."

Ouch.

Debbie and Catherine stood up and walked arm in arm to the house. Catherine kept looking over her shoulder at me like I was some sort of evil demon. Saber went with them, staying by Catherine's side, as if he sensed her need for protection. Buddy continued to harass any rabbit that dared rear its docile head. Until Ben, my semi-adoptive black bear cub, came out of the tree line.

Ben must have been an orphan, because I never saw him with a parent, and he was too young to be on his own. Black bears aren't very common in Eminence, and they're usually docile as long as you don't feed them. I liked having him around, so I did feed him once in a while, but only small snacks over by the tree line.

When Saber first caught a whiff of Ben, he was wary, but not scared. I didn't think Dobermans had a fear gene in their DNA, one of the many reasons I thought the breed special. He and Ben seemed to have developed a mutual respect for each other and stayed out of each other's way.

Buddy wasn't privy to their agreement, and when Ben stood up on his hind legs and started sniffing the air, Buddy forgot all about the rabbits and his moldy chew ball souvenir from Newburgh and ran inside so fast that he whacked the top of his head going through the doggie door. He banged it so hard that the blinds in the whole house rattled. I thought he might be concussed.

A few seconds later, I saw him jump onto the couch. He watched Ben through the living room window, barked at him a few times, and acted all manly now that he was safe inside the house.

I inspected my airplane for damage and I found a small

dent in the leading edge of the wing where we'd taken out the pool ladder. Other than that, my baby was undamaged. Aircraft-grade aluminum is one tough material. I made a mental note to bang that dent out to get rid of all evidence of my Monty Python–like takeoff.

I removed all my weapons and lined them up on my shop bench for cleaning. The slide assembly of the Glock had to go into my meltdown pile, along with the bolt assembly for the Remington. We'd used lead bullets that deformed on impact, so forensics wouldn't be able to link the bullets to our gun barrels, but the shell casings were traceable, and I'd littered them all over the place.

I cleaned out the airplane, refueled her, and tucked her in for a well-deserved rest. My baby'd done good.

29

Cosmo looked at his burner phone and read the cryptic one-word text for the third time.

"Trouble."

"Shit, what the fuck does this mean?" He tossed his phone to Amare, a short, squat fellow who was built like a fridge, and barked instructions. "Get ahold of Dwayne and see what the fuck he's talking about." He shifted on the couch, stuck his hand into one of his pockets, and grabbed another phone. He turned it on and dialed Catherine.

It went straight to voicemail.

"Stupid bitch isn't picking up either." He grabbed the remote and flicked on the TV.

The boarded-up and abandoned house on Bailey Street, just down the street from his very first heroin house, wasn't as nice as his spread in Chairsville, and he missed the tranquility that his golf course provided, but he loved being close to the action. His cash bribes had gotten him a pirated electrical feed and satellite dish on the roof of the house, as well as water service, so he had many of the comforts of home.

Having grown up in Camden, he felt at ease in the run-down neighborhood that he'd taken over. With savvy business skills and a propensity for violence, he'd done well for himself. Unlike many of his long-gone rivals, he saved all the cash he made, watching every penny like an old miser. He didn't waste it on woman and hangers-on. He reinvested it back into the business, although not in the traditional way of modernizing a plant or expanding a sales force.

After a few years of small-time dealing, he'd amassed enough cash to hire a loyal crew of muscle, many of whom were still with him today, and the Silent But Deadly Aces was officially formed. Initiation included performing a drive-by gunning down of a random drug dealer on a South Camden street corner that must result in at least one innocent bystander being killed, and an SBDA tattoo across your chest, or abs if the chest was already spoken for.

If you were a female, your first initiation task, and something that you repeated until perfection was attained, was to blow Cosmo. Depending on your membership status, i.e., how hot you were, you were either kept around to satisfy the male members' sexual demands, or put out on the street to bring in some extra cash. If you had particular attributes, one of them being white skin, you were likely to become one of Cosmo's favorites, which meant that you were off-limits to everyone except Cosmo. He was, however, known to "lend" his favorites out to his friends on a regular basis.

Catherine was one of Cosmo's favorites.

First the SBDA had taken over Bailey Street, Cosmo's old hood where he had grown up, with a single night of violent terror that the locals still whispered about to this day. When the sun had risen the following day, there were eighteen dead bodies, all gunned down in cold blood, lined up on Bailey Street. It looked like a war zone in a fourth-world country.

Nobody in Camden had called the cops when they heard the gunshots, and they wouldn't have arrived until daylight anyway. The local press often listened on the police scanners for the juiciest crimes, and when the airwaves announced a report of multiple homicides on Bailey Street, the press arrived on the scene before the cops did. They started filming, complete with dead bodies littering the streets as their backdrop. This particular reporting team showed up in a modified Humvee made to look like a military machine, and the reporter and camera crew were decked out in the latest military protection gear that reminded all its viewers that they were reporting from a war zone.

The video went viral.

The feds arrived right away, Justice Department officials, state trooper bigwigs, and local politicians all saying the right things to the camera but only succeeding in delivering one thing: lip service.

Fast forward seven years, and Cosmo and the SBDA had expanded from Bailey Street, to York, to Grant, and then to all of Pyne Point. Everything north of I-676 was controlled by Cosmo. Everything south of I-676 was membership initiation fodder.

Amare walked over to Cosmo to deliver the bad news. "Dwayne ain't answering, boss, but you need to see what's on the news."

Cosmo grabbed the remote and turned on CNN.

"Holy fuck."

The live coverage of Cosmo's slaughterhouse started with a helicopter video of the entire property, which was filled with police cars, fire trucks, and ambulances. Narration from an onsite news reporter described the "upscale neighborhood with multimillion-dollar homes." The video zoomed in on the backyard golf course, further in on the torn-up turf, and finally focused on the two sheet-covered bodies sprawled out on the patio, a dark stain seeping out from under them.

Text ran along the bottom of the video that described the body count found inside the house, and how the police were still collecting evidence.

Cosmo took one look at his ripped-up golf course and threw the remote at the TV. He missed, and the remote shattered against the wall. "Motherfucker. Who the hell did this?" He stood up and paced around the room, kicking over the already abused lamps, chairs, and couches. He grabbed his phone and dialed Catherine again. Straight to voicemail.

He turned to Amare. "Call in the crew. We got work to do. And get Locator Larry over here right away. Tell him to bring his equipment. He's gonna earn his money."

"Will do." Amare stepped into the bedroom to make his phone calls and shut the door behind him.

Cosmo dialed Catherine gain. Voicemail. He was starting to worry about her. His informants inside the police department texted him that all the dead bodies in his house were male, and everyone in the house was accounted for. Except Catherine. He also learned that the neighbors reported being awakened by gunshots and a low-flying plane.

For Catherine not to answer his calls, she must be in trouble. In the world that Cosmo existed in, trouble and dead often went hand in hand. Out of all the women in his stable, Catherine was his favorite, and he'd hate to lose her.

Especially to a competitor who'd ruined his golf course.

30

Debbie gave Catherine some of her clothes and set her up in the spare bedroom. She slept most of the day, came out around dinnertime and asked Debbie for some more Advil. She didn't eat anything, or acknowledge me, other than to give me the finger. She got her Advils with a glass of water and went back to her room. Her piercing black eyes were filled with anger, and she spat daggers at me as she slammed the door shut.

Debbie frowned and shook her head. "She looks like shit."

"That's to be expected. She's got a drug addiction, plus she's been through a brutal day. I can't imagine what's going through her mind right now."

"Probably how to escape from us."

"You should think about taking her to a doctor for a

physical. I bet she's got all kinds of health issues going on, plus she'll need some meds to help her ease off the drugs."

"I thought of that. I need to talk to her and see if she's open to it."

"Did she speak to you at all when I was in the hangar?"

"Yeah, she's angry and feels terrible. It sounds crazy, but all those men in her house were her friends. They looked after her, like big brothers. You killed them all and now she hates you for it."

"Unfortunately, I didn't kill them all. None of them were Cosmo."

"She said he wasn't home last night. He spends about half his time in Camden, where he was last night."

"Lucky bastard. Our mission would have been a complete success if he was there."

"No worries, Catherine is safe now."

"Is she? With that psycho running around, nobody is safe."

"How's he ever going to find us?"

"People like that have ways, and they don't give up. It ruins their street cred if they do. And one thing about that Cosmo—he values his street cred above everything else."

"True. But I still think the odds of him tracking us down are slim to none."

"Yeah, well, just the same, I'll keep tabs on him through HFS."

"Good thinking."

We finished our dinner and sat on the couch with a cold beer. I wanted to put on some Barry White, but Debbie nixed that idea. "Yeah, right, I don't think so."

THE NEXT DAY I was up early and left for work before sunrise. The plan was for Debbie to take Catherine to the doctor for a full physical, get her into some kind of drug treatment program, and ease her back into normal life.

Saber's protective instinct made him a good fit for Catherine, and she befriended him right away. He was perfect for her at this point in her life, and what she needed most. A companion who didn't judge you and only wanted to be your friend.

We decided that Catherine would be better off if all three of us stayed at my place for a while. This would give her Saber's companionship, along with a remote enough location where we didn't have to worry about her hitching a ride out of town. She hadn't opened up to me, and might never, but at least she didn't give me the finger anymore.

In between my busy day of handing out speeding tickets and breaking up a parking lot scuffle between two old geezers in the Cobleskill Walmart, I managed to get in some HFS research on Cosmo. Although his past activities were well documented, he'd been off grid for the last few days and nowhere to be found. It was like he'd dropped off the face of the earth. That scared me. If he was smart enough to evade HFS eavesdropping, he was more dangerous than I thought.

Boy, was I ever right.

31

SPECIAL AGENT in Charge Paul Cefalu finished reading the *New York Times* article that Leo Kennedy had emailed him. It was a story of gang violence in Camden, New Jersey, that Leo thought was linked to the Newburgh Massacre.

He rubbed his forehead and ran his fingers through his hair before stopping at the back of his neck and squeezing the tension out. He'd never, in twenty-six years of federal law enforcement, seen multiple instances of this type of violent activity so close together. What the hell was going on in the world?

He shook his head, sighed, and dialed Leo Kennedy's phone. Leo answered on the second ring.

"Kennedy."

"Leo, in my office, please."

"Be right there."

Agent Cefalu didn't waste any time with pleasantries

when Leo stepped into his office. "I read the article, very interesting."

"Did you see the Crazy Pilot YouTube video of the low-flying aircraft taking out the pool ladder?"

"Yeah, I saw that too. You really think Lamburt's involved in this?"

"When the Newburgh carnage occurred, I dismissed him as a suspect, figuring there was no way one man could do all that. But now I'm starting to wonder again. Oh, one other thing I forgot to mention." Leo was almost breathless in his excitement. "Do you remember the complaint from the guy in Kingston? The one who called in about the low-flying aircraft the night Agent Skillman disappeared?"

"Oh yeah, I remember. What about him?"

"He called me this morning. He was one of the sixteen million viewers of that Crazy Pilot YouTube video. He swears it's the same aircraft he saw the night Agent Skillman disappeared."

"I wouldn't pay too much attention to him, Leo. Isn't he close to a hundred years old? And he saw it at night, too."

"Yes, but he's sharp as a tack, and he swears that with the nearly full moon, he could identify the aircraft. That plus the sound of the engine. He's a WWII pilot, and been involved in aviation his whole life. Everything from flying to sales, to maintenance of aircraft. He swears on his great-grandkids that the aircraft he heard was a Cessna 206H with a Power Flow tuned exhaust."

"Interesting. And let me guess, Lamburt owns a..."

Leo nodded his head. "Exactly. A Cessna 206H. With Power Flow tuned exhaust."

Cefalu smiled. "All right, you can keep looking into Lamburt, but not until after we check off all the boxes in this Newburgh investigation. That has to take precedence."

"Roger, sir."

Cefalu jotted down some notes on a legal pad and handed the sheet to Leo. "Two more bodies turned up in a basement in Newburgh. The landlord discovered the remains when he went to fix the washing machine in the basement. Said the door was locked from the inside, had a hell of a time getting in. Interview him and this lady named Mariana, who lives in the building. She claims that she met the man who killed the two guys."

Leo took the note, read it, and stuck it in his pocket. He nodded and left.

32

AFTER A LONG DAY of policing I stopped by the Red Barn, looking forward to having a few cold ones and seeing my Debbie. It was just after happy hour, and the parking lot was almost empty, most of her fans having had their fill of one-dollar beer specials and gone home.

I opened the door and sat down at my usual spot at the bar. Frances waved to me and raised her whiskey glass with a wink and a smile.

I waved back, all the while praying that Debbie would come and rescue me from my biggest fan.

I caught the swinging half doors to the kitchen popping open, and Debbie sped through them, balancing chicken fingers and two icy mugs of beer on a tray. She placed them at a table of two men, had a few words with them, and walked away. Their eyes followed her ass until it was hidden behind the bar. She looked at me and smirked, and I knew that something was wrong.

She brought me over my favorite beverage, a Molson XXX in a frosted mug, and placed it on front of me.

"Thanks." I raised my mug and toasted her.

"We got trouble," she said. "The doctor found a lump in Catherine's breast."

"Oh no."

"I'll say. He took an X-ray, and it's not natural."

"What? What do you mean?"

"He's positive it's a foreign object."

"What the...?"

"Yeah. I had a long talk with her, and it turns out that Cosmo paid for her to have a breast job."

"I knew it! Tits that perfect couldn't—"

She punched me in the shoulder. "Shut up, Patrick. Don't talk about my sister that way."

"Oh, uhm." I shrugged my shoulders and smiled. "Sorry."

"The doc thinks that the foreign object could be a GPS tracking device."

I stopped midswig and looked at her. "Are you messing with me?"

"No."

Damn, that's bad. If the doc was right, the ramifications were gigantic. "So Cosmo could know where she is." I frowned and put my beer down. "This is bad. Did he remove it?"

"No, but he's going to first thing in the morning. She's spending the night in the hospital so the doc can finish running tests on her."

"If Cosmo drives up here tonight, she's a sitting duck. Even with all the HFS firepower, I can't find him. For all we know, he's already on his way up here. Or worse." I stood up and downed the rest of my beer. "He could have a record of everywhere she's been, including my house. And here. I need to get over to the hospital. I'll stay all night and make sure she's safe. You go to my house with Saber and Buddy. Soon as you get there, pop the safe and grab a Glock."

"I'll walk you out."

She gave me a big hug and a kiss in the parking lot. I opened the gun safe bolted to the floor of the extended cab section of my truck, took out two Derringers, and handed them to her. She checked that they were loaded and shoved one in each front pocket. She smiled, kissed me again, and went back inside.

The Derringers would help in a sticky situation, but I was still worried about her safety tonight. Once she got to my house with my Glocks, Saber, and Buddy, she'd be fine. Catherine, on the other hand, was a sitting duck.

I hopped into my pickup and sped over to the hospital in Cobleskill. I drove around the near-empty parking lot a few times looking for out-of-state license plates, but I didn't see any. That was a good sign, but Cosmo and his merry band of assassins could have driven up here, rented a car with fake ID, and be inside killing Catherine right now.

I parked, screwed my Osprey silencer on my Glock, and stuck it in my belt, where it was well hidden under my untucked flannel shirt. I walked over to the entrance and badged my way past the unarmed afterhours security guard, who seemed to be more interested in his smartphone than anything else. I made small talk with the receptionist while she looked up Catherine's room number.

I took the stairs to the third floor two at a time and stepped out into the empty hallway. The lighting was dim and it was eerily silent, about what you'd expect in a quiet small-town hospital at night. I still had to be cautious, though. There was no telling what Cosmo would do. I knew from HFS research that he was a stone-cold killer. He'd been responsible for eighteen murders in a single night and valued his street cred more than anything else in his life. Which meant that if he thought that Catherine had double-crossed him, she was as good as dead.

I eased my way down the hallway until I reached Catherine's room. I didn't knock. I stepped into her room, and my cell phone rang. Shit!

I reached own, grabbed the sides of my iPhone through my pants, and squeezed the silent button. The ringing stopped, and I stood there for a second, listening for a sound, but I didn't hear any. I peered around the privacy curtain that surrounded Catherine's bed. She was sitting up, wide awake, looking right at me, emergency call button in her hand.

"What the hell are you doing here?" She held the call button device in front of her. "Get out, or I'll call for help."

"Easy." I held my hands out, "I'm just here to make sure you're all right."

"I was just dandy until you came along and killed all my friends. You're a freakin' psycho. I could have you thrown in jail. All's I got to do is press this little button." She smirked at me, all proud of her ace in the hole.

I sighed. "I was hoping it wouldn't come to this." I unplugged the end of the emergency call button cord from the wall and tossed it in her lap. I took out my Glock and pressed it against her forehead. I watched as her complexion went from suntanned goddess to white as a ghost. Her eyes got so big she didn't even look half Japanese anymore. She dropped the emergency call button and closed her eyes.

I pushed her backwards with the Glock until she was lying down. She was trembling, her whole body shivering, and sweat had beaded up on her forehead. I stuck the Glock in my belt.

I sat down on the side of the bed and clamped my hand over her mouth. Her skin was cold and clammy. It felt like shaking hands with a dead body. Her eyes shot open, and then she stifled a cry and slammed them shut.

I leaned over and whispered, slow and soft in her ear, "Your sister and I took great risks to rescue you. You might not appreciate it now, but I promise that in due time, you will. Do you understand me?"

She didn't respond.

I leaned away from her and spoke again. "I'm going to remove my hand now so that you and I can have a civilized conversation. Are you going to behave yourself?"

She nodded, and I took my hand away. She opened her eyes and brought her hand up to her mouth to stifle another cry.

"Do you know about the GPS tracking device?"

She nodded.

"The men we took you from know where you are. There's a good chance that they'll come looking for you. I'll make sure that if they do, they die. Do you understand?"

She nodded again, the whole time leaving her hand over her mouth to hold back her cries.

"Good. And another thing. I'm on a mission in life to remove some very bad people from this earth. And no one is going to stop me. Not the police, nor the FBI, and certainly not you. So if I think for a second that you are jeopardizing my life's mission—look at me now, this is important—Debbie's sister or not, I will kill you. No matter where you run, I will track you down, just like I did a few days ago. But instead of carrying you out of a house, I'll kill you inside of it. You saw firsthand what I'm capable of, and that was only the tip of the iceberg. Are we clear on this?"

She turned two shades whiter and nodded, tears gliding down her cheeks and spilling onto her oversized hospital gown.

"Good." I smiled at her, leaned forward, and kissed her

on her forehead. She jumped. I turned to walk away but
stopped in my tracks. "Oh, and one more thing. Stop
scowling at me like I'm Hitler's offspring."

I left Catherine's room, did a cursory walk through the
dim hallway, and went down the stairs and out to my truck.
There were no new vehicles in the parking lot. I climbed
into my pickup and dialed Debbie. She answered on the
first ring. "Hey, baby, everything okay? Catherine safe?"

"Yeah, everything's fine," I told her, deciding to leave out
the part about threatening to kill Catherine. "How about
you? Dogs good?"

"Yeah, one on each side of me, and a Glock in my lap."

"Buddy snoring?"

"Like a buzz saw. I don't know how Saber sleeps with
that racket."

"I'm more worried about you getting a good night's
sleep. We're taking another road trip, and it's going to be a
long couple of days."

"Where to?"

"I'll tell you about it in the morning. We leave right after
Catherine gets out of post-op."

"Who's going to stay with her while we're gone?"

"An old friend, Frankie. I called in a favor."

"Okay, I'll be at the hospital first thing. Kisses."

"Night, baby. Sleep tight." I hung up the phone and went
back into the hospital. When I got to Catherine's room, she
was in the bathroom, so I took a seat and planned my next
set of moves.

Catherine came out of the bathroom and glanced at me with pursed lips. She climbed into bed, turned on her side so her back was to me, and went to sleep.

33

COSMO BARKED out a fast-food order to one of his underlings and tossed him a twenty. "Get some extra fries too."

He turned to Amare. "Who we got? How many?"

"The usual crew, minus the missing-in-action from your house. Seven total."

"That's plenty. When's Locator Larry getting here?"

"Any minute now. He's on his way."

"Good." Cosmo looked at his oversized watch and smiled his gold-toothed grin. "When he confirms her location for us, I'm sending men right away. Make sure they're ready to go when they get here. I don't want any delays."

"Okay, boss man."

As if on cue, a small balding old white man pulled up in a Toyota hybrid.

Amare spotted him through the front window. "Larry's here, boss man."

Cosmo hoisted himself off the couch and walked over to look out the window. He watched as the little old man stepped out of his car, opened his rear hatch, and took out a briefcase. "What a sorry excuse for a man. Think he ever gets laid?"

"I don't know, boss, probably not. Maybe you can help him out."

"Yeah, right, I don't think so. Every one of my whores would kill his skinny white ass by the end of the night."

Cosmo leaned over the railing and yelled down to his door man. "Yo, Pauly, Larry's here. Send him up."

"Will do, boss."

A few seconds later, Cosmo heard the old man enter the house and shuffle his way up the stairs. When he reached the top, he took out a handkerchief and wiped the sweat from his face. "Hello, Mr. Cosmo. I understand you want to locate one of your assets?"

"That's right, Larry. I need to find somebody. Right now."

"Very well." The old man walked over to the table in the kitchen, laid his briefcase on top of it, and popped the two latches. He took out a laptop and turned it on.

"Who are we finding, Mr. Cosmo?"

"Catherine."

The little old white man adjusted his glasses and went to work, banging fingertips on his laptop until he looked up with a smile. "I've found her."

"Where is she?"

"As of six hours ago, she was in a little town in upstate NY called Summit."

"Six hours ago? Shit, she could be in Canada by now."

"Unlikely. This is a quiet little town, and I'm guessing she'll be there for a while."

"I don't pay you to guess. I'm sending some men to get her back. You go with them in case she makes a run for it before they get there."

"I'm afraid that's not possible, Mr. Cosmo. Travel is not included in my duties, and I have responsibilities here that I must attend to."

Cosmo took out his pistol and pressed it against the old man's forehead. "Don't make me fuckin' shoot you. You're going. You understand?"

The old man's eyes grew so wide he looked like he'd witnessed the second coming of Christ. His jaw fell open and he looked down at the floor. His whole body started shaking. Cosmo thought he was going to have a stroke. He couldn't afford to lose him and his tracking software, so he put the gun away and changed his tone to a friendlier one. "Just get her and bring her back. I'll make it worth your while."

The old man didn't answer.

"Help him out to the car, Amare. They can take the SUV. And tell Vargas to get his ass up here."

Amare grabbed the old man under the arm and hoisted him up. "Come on, old man, let's go."

"Larry. My name's Larry." He folded up his laptop, stuck it in his briefcase, and followed Amare.

Vargas came running up the stairs. The former high school football player, still in shape in his midtwenties, took the steps three at a time. "You wanted to see me, boss?"

"Yeah, take Larry and find Catherine. I know she had something to do with the attack on my crib. Bring her back alive. I want to make her suffer myself."

"You got it, boss."

Cosmo reached into a kitchen drawer and took out a burner cell phone. "Here, take this. My burner phone number is the only one in the contacts. Keep me updated on your progress, but only use *this* phone to text me. Take JA with you."

"You got it, boss." Vargas ran down the steps, called out for JA, and headed out the door.

34

THEY CAME to get Catherine at six sharp and wheeled her off to surgery. Debbie showed up just in time to give her a hug and a good luck kiss.

We went to get breakfast at a nearby diner and came back and sat in the waiting room. A few hours later, the doc came out with a smile on his face. "Everything is fine. She did good. Implants were removed, along with the foreign object."

"Thanks, Doc. When can I have the foreign object? I'm anxious to start my investigation."

"Any minute now. I ordered the nurse to clean it up and bring it out to you."

"Thanks again for your help, Doc. I owe you one." I winked and shook his hand. He smiled back at me.

We sat down and waited for the nurse. Fifteen minutes

later, she came out and handed me a container with the object inside. We thanked her and left.

We sat in my truck and opened the container to look at the object. It looked like a big horse pill with some numbers etched in the side. I'd researched it through HFS and knew exactly what it was. "Yep. It's a GPS tracking device all right. It sends out a signal to the nearest satellite. It's crazy that Cosmo tracks his women this way. I guess he has a high turnover rate."

"You think? What an animal. So now what?"

"Put it in your bag. We'll take the tracking device on our little road trip. Cosmo will come looking for us, and we'll let him find us. On our terms."

"What about Catherine? What if he shows up here after we've left?"

"I called in a favor. From one of my good friends from my NSA days, Frankie, who went on to become a CIA operative."

"What kind of operative?"

"Assassin. Close-up. Knife, strangulation, that sort of thing."

"Excellent! When's he get here?"

"Frankie's a she, as in Francesca."

"Oh. How well do you know her?"

I looked at her and shrugged.

Her eyes grew narrow. "You were lovers? You called up an old lover, to watch your current lover's sister?" She punched me in the arm. "Explain yourself!"

"What's to explain? I met her on the coed volleyball team at NSA."

"She plays volleyball?"

"I don't think she plays anymore. She was good too. Went to the Olympic trials for beach volleyball when she was in college."

"Beach volleyball? That's the one with the girls in skimpy bikinis."

"Yeah, that's the one."

"And you guys were lovers."

"Yeah, but we haven't seen each other in years. She's a good operative, and I trust her to make sure that nothing happens to Catherine. She's posing as Catherine's sister, by the way."

"What? Wait... her sister, Debbie? As in me? Your old lover is posing as me?"

"It was the only way I could get her hospital access without raising any eyebrows."

"Does she at least look like me?"

"Not really."

"Then how's she going to pose as me? The doc knows me, Patrick."

"Doc's in on it. He'll play along, official police matter and all." I winked at her.

She punched me in the arm again. "You suck, Jack Lamburt." She crossed her arms over her chest and looked out the passenger window.

I opened my door, stepped out, and leaned against the truck to wait for Frankie.

Five minutes later, and it was a long five minutes with Debbie pouting, Frankie pulled up in her light blue BMW M3 and parked next to me. She smiled, took off her sunglasses, and walked over to me. She looked great. Long muscular legs that ended in a tan miniskirt. A halter top that showed off her abs, tattoos, and muscular shoulders, and a wide smile that reminded me how easy it was for her to get close enough to her targets to kill them.

"Well, hello, Jack Lamburt. Long time no see."

I held out my hand. She smiled and playfully smacked it away. I was afraid of that.

"Really? That's how you're going to greet an old lover?" She threw her arms around me, kissed me on the cheek, and gave me a long, tight hug.

"Ahem." Debbie had gotten out of my truck and was standing with her arms crossed, glaring at us.

"Frankie, this is Debbie." I pointed to her. "Debbie, Frankie."

"Nice to meet you."

"Thanks, you too," Debbie replied, icicles hanging from every word.

"Wow, she's as beautiful as you said. You done good, Jack." Frankie walked all over Debbie with her eyes and smiled at me. "Yeah. You were right. I'd do her," she added with a nod.

"Excuse me?" Debbie voice rose an octave.

"You're hot. I'd do you. It's a compliment."

Debbie glared at me. "This is what you guys talked about? How hot I am?"

"It's an old habit of ours." *Oh crap.* I regretted saying that as soon as the words left my lips. Goddamn impulse control issues...

"Wait, you guys used to pick up women together?"

Frankie and I just looked away, down at our feet, at our watches.

"I don't believe this. You never told me that you and your old girlfriend were womanizers."

"The subject never came up."

"I don't have time for this right now," She turned to Frankie. "Will you take care of Catherine for us?"

"Debbie. That's *why* she's here."

Frankie looked at me and smiled. "It's okay, Jack. I'm guessing that she doesn't know the bond that agents form."

"Bond that agents form?" Debbie asked.

Frankie turned to Debbie. "No one will get to Catherine without killing me first, and I can assure you, that's not going to happen. Now you two go take care of business." She reached into her car and grabbed her purse, "When she's discharged, I'll take her back to Jack's place and stay with her until you get back." She turned and asked me, "Garage code still the same?"

Oh crap, I wished she hadn't asked me that in front of Debbie. "Yep. There's plenty of food in the fridge, and all my weapons are locked up in the gun safe. Saber and Buddy have a doggie door, so they let themselves out. They have automatic feeders, and their water bowls are automatically filled when they decline to a certain level, so they're self-reliant."

I thought I was slick, changing the subject about the garage code by going over what I had already briefed Frankie on.

Debbie would have none of it. I felt her daggers slicing through my back and turned and delivered my best lady-killer smile. She looked at me, her almond-shaped eyes morphing into tight little slits, and scoffed.

"She knows the garage code?" She shook her head and pursed her lips. "Boy, do you have some explaining to do when this is over."

35

WE CLIMBED INTO MY PICKUP, and I drove over to I-88 and headed east. Other than asking where we were going, to which I replied, "Peru, New York," Debbie was quiet for the first forty minutes or so. After we hit the New York State Thruway in Albany and headed north, she switched over to her usual self. "So what's the plan, Stan?"

"Dad's family owned a property in Peru that was used as an Underground Railroad stop. I haven't been there in a while, but I spent a lot of time there as a kid. Dad loved teaching us about the role that the farm played in the Underground Railroad."

"Underground Railroad, as in helping the slaves escape captivity?"

"Yeah, this place goes back a long time and has a ton of history. Complete with tunnels that the slaves traveled by. I used to play in them when I was a kid. It's the perfect place to lure Cosmo."

"You think he'll drive all the way up there? Maybe we should have headed south, closer to him, to entice him to visit us."

"All my HFS research on Cosmo indicates that he'll track Catherine down, even if she's on Mars."

"What do we do when we get there?"

"We set up an ambush. The old stone farmhouse is built like a fort and surrounded by hundreds of acres of forest. There's only one way in, and one way out, so they can't sneak up on us."

The one-hundred-and-eighty-four-mile trip took us a little over three hours. We didn't stop anywhere, and I paid all tolls in cash. I had put all of our phones and my E-ZPass in a lead-shielded bag so that we were untraceable.

Once we arrived, I found the trail to the house overgrown with tall grass and an occasional shrub, but I had no problem getting through with my pickup. I pulled up to the house and was immediately hit with flashbacks of running through the woods with my cousins as a kid. Good times.

We got out, and Debbie was the first to speak. "Wow, this is desolate. Makes Eminence look like New York City."

"Nobody around for many miles."

"You weren't kidding about it being a fortress either." She pointed to the steel shutters that were over every window, locked in place from the inside.

"Dad figured that was the best way to keep the animals and stray folks out of the house."

I reached into my truck, grabbed my go bags and went up to the front door. "Aw shit." I looked at Debbie.

"What?" she asked.

"I forgot the key."

36

Vargas guided the big SUV along the New Jersey Turnpike, and settled in for the long ride to upstate New York. The two-hundred-and-forty-four-mile trip would take him over four hours, and that was without stopping to refuel and stretch his legs. The trip was short notice, so other than his pistol, he hadn't had time to pack, and he'd have to stop for food and water. Plus the old dude Larry sitting in the backseat would probably need to take a piss at least two or three times before they got there.

His thoughts turned to John Anthony, and he wondered if the kid would come through under pressure. Other than handing out a few street beatings, which he did well, Vargas had never seen the kid in action. He'd have to watch him close.

He eyed the old white guy in the rearview mirror. He

was sitting in the second row and typing away on his laptop. "Yo, Lar, where's she now?"

"The last signal is still in Eminence. I'm trying to ping the unit to get an updated location, but this is an older model, and I'm having trouble reaching it. Once I do, I should be able to upgrade the firmware, and it will autosend every couple of hours. Cosmo will be able to follow her on his laptop as well."

Larry's work with the CIA was legendary. He'd led a team of engineers that created the latest in implanted tracking devices, also known as ITDs. Various models of ITDs were implanted inside every prisoner released from Guantanamo Bay and all of the other secretive CIA prisons. Most of the devices were surgically implanted deep in the buttock muscle. A small slit was made in the crease where the butt meets the back of the evildoer's leg using an arthroscopic surgery instrument, and the ITD was placed under the muscle.

Larry had six hundred and fifty-seven ITDs all over the Middle East, and his success rate for tracking individuals was one hundred percent, leading to his nickname of Locator Larry. While he felt pride in his nickname, he'd often stated to his few friends in the Agency that his greatest accomplishment was developing a battery that was trickle-charged by body heat, which gave the module a lifespan of eighteen years.

Larry's career with the Agency had come to an abrupt end when he'd been forced to resign in disgrace after being caught in an intimate relationship with an Asian woman who'd turned out to be a North Korean spy. His only saving grace was that he had never spoken to her about work, so he was cleared of every charge that the Agency brought against him. Except of being gullible, towards which the Agency had a zero-tolerance policy. Was it that hard to believe that a woman twenty years his junior could find him interesting and fall in love with him? He could, after all, complete the *New York Times* crossword puzzle in under thirty minutes...

Larry had no idea that his lover had deceived him on every level, and in addition to being booted from the Agency after twenty-nine years of otherwise excellent service and having his heart broken, he'd had his pension taken away.

After wallowing in alcohol-fueled self-pity for a few months, he had run out of money and decided to get his act together. He'd started his own business manufacturing tracking modules for pet owners. The only problem was that pet owners didn't want to pay for the high cost of his modules just to track down a runaway pet.

But possessive husbands did. That discovery had led him to develop a breast implant module to go along with the butt version, and the two became a huge hit amongst the insecure husbands with cash to spare. And there were plenty of them. They loved Larry and his team of corrupt docs. Not only did they get bigger tits to salivate over, they got to keep track of them too.

His initial introduction to Cosmo had raised a few red

flags, but that was early in his new career, when he was broke. And desperate. And desperate men do desperate things, so he'd caved in and offered his services to Cosmo.

He'd found out later that Cosmo was worse than he'd imagined. He wasn't just a stone-cold killer. He'd executed one of his street dealers right in front of him and seven other men who were meeting with him inside one of his crack houses. He'd sent the body down to the basement to be hacked up and fed to his twin Rottweilers. He loved commenting that you "can't get reliable DNA from dog shit." Cosmo liked sending messages, and this message was clear. "I kill people, and feed 'em to my dogs."

The earlier version of Larry's GPS tracking module—the one hidden in Catherine's and two other girls' implants—required a complicated computer program that only Larry could run on his laptop. The newer versions had a much simpler program that any hood, or husband, could use, but try as he might, he couldn't get Cosmo to "upgrade" the implant and free himself from his in-person duties. "What are you, fucking crazy? How am I gonna convince my girls that they need a breast implant upgrade? They're dumb bitches, but not that stupid."

He had thought of killing the three women, which would put an end to Cosmo's need to have him track them, but he'd decided the risk wasn't worth it. He'd gamble and hope that none of the three would run off before he upgraded them with new software, but his new software was overrun with bugs and it had taken longer to fix then he thought. And he couldn't rush it. It had to be perfect before he upgraded, because if it crashed and he lost a girl, holy crap, he'd have hell to pay.

His extensive testing was why the upgraded software was still in beta version and hadn't been used in real life. Until now. He logged in, said a quick prayer, and hit the firmware upgrade button.

Vargas turned down the hip-hop on the radio. "Where she at, Larry? Still in Eminent?"

"Eminence. No, I logged in and upgraded the software. I just received a ping from Peru."

"Peru? I ain't going to fuckin Europe. Hey, JA, you ever been to Europe?"

"Nah, man, never been outside a' Jersey. You?"

"Hell yeah, bro, I've been to Philly many times." He stuck his chest out.

Larry looked up from his laptop and shook his head. "The signal came from Peru, New York, a little town up near Canada. I'll give you directions in a minute."

37

DEBBIE'S MOUTH dropped open in shock. "What? What do you mean you forgot the key? Like, 'we can't get in the house' forgot your key?"

"Yeah."

She rolled her eyes. "I can't believe I let you sleep with me."

"I was in a rush."

"So, what now? We can't break into this fort, and if we can't get in, our whole plan is shot to hell."

"I could find one of the old tunnels and crawl my way into the basement."

"Would they still be there after all these years? I mean, wouldn't they collapse over time?"

"Maybe, but I'll never know unless I find one and crawl down it."

I shivered at the thought of that. On my last journey into

one of the tunnels when I was a kid, my friends had jumped up and down on the ground above me to scare me. The dirt had started falling on me, and I'd thought the whole thing was going to cave in and bury me alive. I'd panicked and freaked out, started yelling and screaming for them to stop, but they hadn't. I'd hauled ass out of that tunnel like I was on fire and hadn't been back since.

"You remember where the entrances are?"

"I could probably find one." I could never forget, even if I wanted to.

"What about the basement door? Won't it be locked?"

"Yeah." I patted my Glock. "But those locks are old and flimsy. I can blast my way through them."

"What about blasting your way through the front door?"

"I could, but then we wouldn't be able to lock it behind us. I'd feel much better being able to secure it."

"I guess you're right. Let's go, then. We don't have any time to waste. As far as we know, Cosmo could be on his way right now."

I led Debbie to the backyard and into the tree line. It took me about thirty seconds to find the tunnel entrance, which was an old wooden door that was rotten and caved in, leaving a big hole to the tunnel entrance. I grabbed what was left of the door, swung it open, and laid it on the forest floor.

The smell of damp dirt brought flashbacks of my friends doing the elephant dance over my head. I tried to swallow, but my throat was too dry. Crap. I shook my head and scoffed at the ridiculousness of my nerves. Hell, I'm a bad-ass who kills people. I'm not scared of a freaking tunnel. I took a deep breath and looked at my house to measure the distance. It couldn't have been more than sixty or seventy feet. Not even a stone's throw. Piece of cake.

"Wow, that door hasn't done much good keeping the critters out." Debbie leaned forward, peered into the dark tunnel, and grimaced. "Good luck in there. I can't imagine what kind of creepy things fell in there. Spiders and snakes and rats, oh my!" She patted me on the back and smiled. "Don't worry, honey, if the tunnel caves in on you, I'll be sure to give Frankie the news in person. And I'm taking the dogs." She laughed. "Just sayin'..."

I got down on my hands and knees and crawled in. Once I was a few feet from the entrance, I lost the outside light, and the tunnel was pitch black. And silent. My iPhone and its flashlight were still in my lead-shielded bag in my truck, so I was on my own. I closed my eyes and moved through the tunnel a foot at a time.

The air was damp and stale, and I wondered if the lack of fresh air would asphyxiate me. What if there were a long, slow methane leak that filled up the tunnel? Methane gas has no odor and is deadly. Miners used to use canaries in a cage as a methane detector. When the canary died, time to get the hell out. I envisioned a smiling Debbie breaking the news to Frankie that I'd been suffocated or buried alive, and "Oh, by the way, the garage door code had been changed."

Focus!

I shook away the negativity and took a deep breath.

I could feel my back scraping across the top of the tunnel, and I felt little clumps of dirt falling from it as I made progress. The tunnel was too narrow to turn around in, so if I came across a cave-in or other obstruction, like tree roots that had grown through it over the years, I'd have to back my way out.

My vivid imagination got the best of me, and I envisioned bumping my forehead against the butt of a hibernating black bear. All thoughts of the cave-in were replaced by wondering how cranky a disturbed bear would be. That was a childish distraction, though, just to take my mind off my real fears, because hibernation season was over.

It was now... oh crap...

Cub season.

I envisioned plowing into a bear cub, scaring the bejesus out of it and making it squeal in fright. The mother bear, who was out foraging for food, hears the cry of help from its little angel. She comes barreling into the tunnel to rescue her baby.

Now my exit's blocked, and even if I shot her to save myself from her attack, I still wouldn't be able to get out of the tunnel because there was no way that I could push a four-hundred-pound bear out of the tunnel.

Every time I felt my anxiety rise, I focused on my breathing, and that helped keep my demons at bay. Until a vision of a nest of copperheads or timber rattlesnakes fought its way into my head, biting me thousands of times before I could back out.

I should cut down on my caffeine intake.

I must have been subconsciously counting out my baby steps, because I felt the roof of the tunnel rise just as I was thinking that I should be getting close to the basement door.

I reached a small open area where I could kneel up straight, which felt good on my back. There was a tiny sliver of light coming in along the door frame, which must be coming in the basement through the screened-in air vents on the basement wall just above the ground. As the proverbial light at the end of the tunnel, it wasn't much, but I was relieved to see it.

I touched the wooden door and fumbled around for the doorknob. I found it, the cool metal returning normalcy to my dirt-overloaded brain. I turned it, but it wouldn't budge. I sighed and took out my Glock. I fumbled around for the silencer, found it, and after four attempts, I managed to start the thread correctly and screw it on.

I leaned it against the doorknob, closed my eyes, and fired. Even with the silencer the Glock was loud, and I could see a flash of bright light through my closed eyelids.

I inhaled the cordite and smiled at the instant relaxation provided by the comforting familiarity of it. I pushed open the door and crawled into the basement, and into the biggest spiderweb I'd ever seen...

38

THE ENORMOUS SPIDERWEB covered the top half of the doorway and was stretched tight by the door opening. When I stood up into it, it felt like I was stretching a gigantic Ace bandage. It was so strong that it stopped my forward progress for a split second before I forced myself through it and fell into the basement.

There's only one type of spider in upstate New York that can make a web like this.

A black widow.

The female black widow spider loves seclusion, and rarely leaves its web. It prefers to stand guard over its eggs, and although bites from the black widow are rarely fatal to a healthy adult, they hurt like hell. When I plowed into the web, I took it down, egg sac and all.

I hoped that the momma spider would run for the hills, but I knew better. She'd be mad as heck at my demolition of her hard work, not to mention taking her eggs away from her. I had no idea where she was. I brushed off as much of the sticky web as I could and stripped down to my birthday suit just in case the black widow was in my clothes. I ran up the stairs to the first floor. With all the windows shuttered, it was dark, but there was enough light leaking in to find the front door. I opened it and let Debbie in.

She looked me up and down and made a face. "You're disgusting. Grow up."

She elbowed her way past me and I closed the door. "I ran into a black widow web, and I wanted to make sure that she didn't bite me."

"Where's your clothes?"

"Basement, but watch out for the spider."

Debbie went downstairs and I heard her shaking out my clothes. She came up the stairs and threw them at me. "Put your clothes on and quit fooling around. You've wasted enough time." Boy, was she cranky...

She started unpacking the go bags and laying out the weapons on a table in the kitchen. I threw on my clothes and opened the shuttered windows. The house had a stale, hadn't-been-used-in-ten-years odor to it, and it felt good to let the fresh mountain air in.

I went into the kitchen and found one of the propane lanterns in the cupboard and lit it. One was enough to light up the kitchen, and I lit another for the living room.

I grabbed my portable motion detection system, went outside, and placed the sensors around the perimeter of the property. This would alert me to Cosmo and his men as soon as they broke the infrared beam.

When I got back inside the house, I opened my laptop and logged in to the motion detectors via Bluetooth to check the system. I was close enough so that the reception was strong, and I got green lights all around verifying the unbroken beams of infrared light.

I turned to Debbie. "Motion detection's a go. We all set with weaponry?"

She nodded.

The basis of our plan was to make Cosmo believe that Catherine was in the house, in which case he would likely attack at night.

We, of course, would be ready for him. Our base of operations would be an old wooden shed to the side of the house. From that position, we could see the entire approach to the front of the house. We would stake out the house from there, taking turns, four hours at a time. When Cosmo arrived, we would kill the bastard.

I thought about using a deer stand for my end of the stakeout, but I hated being up in a tree and immobile. Things happened fast in a firefight, and I didn't want to be stuck in a tree and locked in to one position, so I opted for the shed instead. Our plan was simple. We'd take turns keeping watch until we heard them approach or they set off one of the perimeter sensors. We'd kill them and drive them down to the Tahawus Quarry lakes, where we could dump them in over a thousand feet of water.

I'd flown over Tahawus some time ago, and as soon as I'd seen the two lakes, I'd had a good feeling they'd come in handy someday. A little bit of research on Google had proven my initial thoughts correct.

The Tahawus Quarry lakes weren't like most lakes, where you could wade in and it gradually deepened. Those lakes were impossible to hide a car in. You'd be lucky to get it submerged a few feet before it stopped rolling, and even if you did manage to get it totally submerged, it was only a matter of time before some unfortunate swimmer broke their neck diving off of their boat into what was supposed to be ten feet of water. Bingo, bodies found.

Not so with Tahawus. These were man-made lakes from the mining and quarry operation, and they had cliffs that went straight down into the water. Pull one of the rock barriers away, push their vehicle over the side, and bye-bye, Cosmo and his clowns. I was confident that there was no way that he was escaping his just fate this time.

I was wrong...

39

FRANKIE WALKED into the hospital and up to the front desk. "I'm here to see Catherine Macintyre. I'm her sister."

The young girl behind the computer screen typed in a few lines, looked up at Frankie, and pointed to a sign-in book. "She's out of post-op and in room 242."

Frankie signed Debbie's name and took the stairs two at a time until she reached the landing. Old habits die hard. She pulled the door open slowly, one hand on the pistol in her purse, and peered around the hallway before stepping out. It was empty. She saw the sign on the wall pointing her in the right direction, and she made her way down the hallway to Catherine's room. She nearly ran into the doctor while he was leaving her room.

"Oh, pardon me," he said.

"I'm Catherine's sister. How's she doing, Doc?"

He paused, a look of mild confusion on his face, and

then smiled knowingly. "Oh, right. Her sister. She's doing excellent. Better than I anticipated. She's resting now, a little groggy from the pain meds we just gave her."

"When will I be able to take her home?"

"Pretty soon. I have a few more test results that have to come back, and then she's all yours. Before you leave, the nurse will go over her medication schedule with you."

"Thanks, Doc. I'll be waiting in here with her."

She turned and sat down by Catherine's bed. The other bed in the room, by the window, was empty and neatly made. The curtains were open and, wary of a sniper attack, she went over and closed them.

There were no machines or wires connected to Catherine, and she checked her pulse to make sure she was still alive. Jack had given her a thorough briefing, and she knew full well how ruthless people like Cosmo could be.

Catherine's skin was warm to the touch, which was a good sign. Frankie felt a sense of relief when she detected a strong and steady pulse. She studied Catherine's face. Even with her eyes closed and no makeup on, Frankie could see the remnants of past beauty. And sadness. *What causes people to go down this path?*

She poured some water from a plastic jug into a cup for when Catherine woke up, and waited. Over two hours went by before Catherine started to stir. She turned onto her side and opened her eyes. She seemed to have trouble focusing on Frankie.

"Hi, Catherine. I'm Frankie."

"Jack told me about you. Where's Debbie?"

"They went on a little road trip. I'll take you back to Eminence when you're discharged. Should be soon. Doc says you're doing well."

"I feel like shit."

"Yeah, that's to be expected. Want some water?" Frankie held out a cup.

"God, yeah, but I'd really love a beer." She took the water and drank it all in one long swig.

"Ha, not until we get you back to Eminence. But you have to promise not to tell Jack. He's a real stickler for following the rules."

Catherine scoffed. "I don't think so. Since I've met him, he's broken all of them."

"He must really care for you. He only breaks the rules for important people in his life."

"How well do you know him?"

"Well. Very well. And for a long time. He's a good man."

"He seems like a psycho killer to me."

"He's not a psycho."

The doctor knocked on the door frame with his knuckles and tried to be funny. "Anybody home?" He stepped into the room, a big smile on his chubby face as he looked at Frankie. He nodded at her. She smiled her best fake smile, the one that she usually reserved for luring targets into her web.

"I have the results of your blood work. Everything came

out well enough for you to be discharged, but it's important that you take all of your meds on schedule."

He looked at Frankie and smiled again. "Can you make sure that she does that?"

Frankie's fake smile parted her lips, and she nodded. "Yes, Doc, I'll make sure." *Now can we get the hell out of here?*

"Good." He turned to Catherine. "I'll need to see you in a few days. Call the office in the morning and make an appointment." He turned to Frankie. "Will you be bringing her in?"

"Yes, Doc, I'll bring her in."

"Good." He stuck out his hand, and Frankie took it. "It was a pleasure meeting you."

She smiled. "You too, Doc. Thanks for all your help with this."

"No problem. I owe Jack big-time."

Forty minutes later, Frankie helped Catherine into her M3, and thirty minutes after that, she punched in the code to Jack's garage.

Frankie knew about Saber and Buddy and didn't want to take any chances, so she asked Catherine to enter the house first. They were both excited to see her, Saber with his stoic demeanor and a little tail-wagging. Buddy was going rambunctious apeshit, running circles around them and holding his toy out for them to try and take away from him. After a couple of minutes of no takers, he disappeared and ran roughshod through the rest of the house.

Saber stayed right next to Catherine.

40

VARGAS SLOWED the big SUV as they got off the New York State Thruway and paid cash for the toll. "Which way, Larry?"

"Right on 9W, left on Pine, left on Route 41."

"Whoa. Right on what?"

"Right on 9W."

"Got it."

Larry gave him turn-by-turn directions unit they arrived at the entrance to the big property. "You better wake your friend up. We'll be there soon."

Vargas elbowed JA. "Wake up, Sleeping Beauty. Freakin' showtime."

JA stirred and rubbed his eyes, then took out his pistol and made sure it had a live round in the chamber. "We're just killing everyone, right?"

Vargas frowned. "Yeah, I ain't bringing that silly bitch all the way to New Jersey. We'll just tell Cosmo that we had no choice."

"He's gonna be pissed."

"He'll be fine. Ain't like he cared about her or anything." He looked in the rearview mirror. "Hey, Larry, you got our back on this, right?"

"Yeah, sure, fellas."

Vargas frowned at the old man's unconvincing comment. "Don't fuck with us, Larry."

"No, no, it's all good. I'm not going to see anything anyway. You guys just take care of business and let's get the hell out of here. There should be a driveway on the right side in about two hundred feet. Pull in there, far enough up so no one can see the taillights from the road. Then you two should walk the rest of the way. There's a house about a half mile up the road. She's in that house."

Vargas slowed down and made a right turn into what looked like an overgrown trail. He crawled about forty feet and saw a chain stretched across the driveway. He stopped and got out, undid the chain and hopped back in. He pulled up another hundred feet, stopped the SUV, and killed the engine.

They sat there in silence for a minute before Vargas broke the tranquility. "Okay, JA, it's time to go. We'll take our time going up the road. Once I get a good look at the house, I'll decide how we go in."

JA nodded. "Got it. Hey, if she's in there by herself, can we have a little fun with her before we do her?"

Vargas laughed, "You mean do her before you do her?"

"Yeah, I ain't never banged the bitch."

Larry spoke up from the backseat. "Come on, you guys, this isn't a party. Just get the job done, and let's go home."

Vargas looked at Larry. "Relax, man, we got it." He smacked JA on the arm. "Come on, bro, let's do this."

They got out of the SUV and walked up the driveway.

41

DEBBIE and I took turns watching the dimmed display of the laptop and using the night vision binoculars to keep a watch out over the overgrown driveway. I knew these guys weren't that smart, and with Catherine's implanted GPS device sitting in the house on the kitchen table, I was sure they'd sneak up through the driveway, see a few lanterns lit, and approach the house.

As soon as I saw them and confirmed them as enemy combatants, I would shoot them. My brand-new Remington 700 was scoped in and ready to go. I could've very easily given Debbie the sniping task, but I hadn't had my fill of killing these evildoers, so I was chomping at the bit.

I left the door to the shed ajar so that Debbie could look out with her night vision binoculars. She sat on the floor, Indian-style, and never took her eyes off of the driveway.

I slid open the only window and kneeled in front of it,

my rifle with night vision scope and flash suppressor leaning against the wall, chambered and ready to fire.

We sat inside the shed in silence most of the night, the boredom and fatigue of long hours enveloping me. I found myself yawning and dozing off on a regular basis, awakened by my falling head hitting my chest, or more often, a cramp in my legs. I'd stand and stretch every once on awhile, but the truth was that I was getting too old for the long hours involved in this kind of stakeout. I silently vowed that from now on, I would never wait for anyone to come to me. I would figure out a way to find them and kill them on my terms.

I love math, so to entertain myself, I started adding up how many hours I'd been without real sleep and converting that to minutes. I was so fatigued that I had a hard time with the simple calculation, something that a grammar school kid could figure out in ten seconds. That wasn't good. Fatigue slows the reflexes, and I couldn't afford to be slow on the draw. I toyed with the idea of taking a power nap, but before I could mention it to Debbie, one of the green sensor lights on the laptop turned yellow.

My adrenaline spiked and every nerve was alive. No more need for a nap. I sat on edge, my eyes glued to the laptop screen, but nothing changed. Could just be a false alarm.

A second light turned yellow. We might have something. The first one turned red, and I knew we had them, or a deer. I rose up on my knees, fully awake from the excitement that a fresh kill shot brought me, and nudged Debbie with my foot.

"I think they're here. The infrared beam next to the driveway just went off. Let me know what you see."

"Roger."

I panned the area with my night vision scope but came up empty.

"Tallyho," Debbie whispered. "Two targets. Confirmed armed. Two pistols. One o'clock and closing in on the house."

I scoped over to my one o'clock position and found them. They were crouched over and making their way through the overgrown driveway, their attention riveted on the house. I steadied my aim, waited for the right moment, and squeezed the trigger between heartbeats. The big rifle fired a lead slug at over two thousand feet per second and nailed the first guy dead center. He flew backwards, dead before he hit the ground. The bullet must have hit the second guy too, because he screamed like a bitch and went down hard. A twofer!

Even Debbie was impressed. "Wow, good shot. I think you got both of them."

I was busy mentally patting myself on the back when she interrupted. "Strike that, second target's on the move."

"What?"

"Get in the game, Patrick. He's on the run. Shoot him before he reaches cover behind the tree line!"

I brought my rifle up, but by the time I found him and fired, he was gone.

"Did I get him?"

"No, I don't think so. Time for a manhunt. Let's go." She whipped open the door and took off after him. I scoped out the tree line, hoping to locate his position, but came up empty. I heard a shot ring out, and Debbie stopped in her tracks and fell to the ground.

My heart froze when I saw her go down. Was she hit? Did she go down to avoid further fire? I didn't hear her scream or groan, which was a good sign.

Unless she got shot right through the heart...

Oh. Shit.

42

Leo sat down in Agent Cefalu's office and sighed. "What now, sir?"

"I don't know what the hell is going on out there, Leo, but we got more bad news. You're not going to believe this, but all the recent killings were done with lead bullets. Every single one that evidence gathering recovered, and there were a lot of them, was deformed lead. No more use to ballistics then a musket ball from the Revolutionary War."

"Do you think the gangs have discovered how hard it is to trace a lead bullet and now they're all using them? If that's the case, we're going to have a hard time gaining convictions with ballistics to back us up."

"I know, but why now?"

"Of course, we might be giving the gangs too much credit. It could be the work of one person, or a small team."

"You're thinking of Lamburt again, aren't you?"

"You have to admit, sir, it's a possibility. Have you noticed that all of the deceased are men?"

"Yes, I have. But we can't get caught up just focusing on him. How'd you make out in Newburgh?"

"The building landlord was no help. He didn't know the two dead men. Or at least that's what he claimed. The method of securing the basement door was ingenious, though. Paracord connected to the inside of the doorknob, looped over a massive pipe in the basement ceiling, and run up the hinged side of the door and knotted. Way too much thinking and effort involved for it to be gang-related."

"What about Mariana Gondoza?"

"Ah, yes, the lady who claimed to have seen the killer. She was stoned when I got there, offered to sleep with me for ten dollars, and when I declined, she moved on to Blake. I don't know about that guy. If I hadn't been there, he might have taken her up on her offer."

"She offer you anything worthwhile?"

"Not really. She gave a rough description." Leo pulled out his iPhone, tapped on the Evernote app, and read the description. "Tall short-haired white guy. Big muscles. Nice bulge in his pants." He shrugged his shoulders at Cefalu. "Her words, not mine."

"That's it?"

"Yeah. I thought about returning with a photo of Lamburt, but she's an addict and I view her statements as completely unreliable."

"Did you find any other witnesses?"

"Negative, sir. Typical high-crime neighborhood with residents unwilling to talk to the FBI or the local police. Nobody saw anything about anything."

"I figured that. Okay, keep moving forward with what you have. Dismissed."

"Will do, sir."

43

IN A PANIC I dropped my rifle and ran to Debbie's side. I dove on the ground next to her and grabbed her arm. "Debbie, you okay? Debbie?"

Gunshots rang out, and I hugged her tight, pulling her in close to me to shield her.

"Shut up, Patrick, I'm fine," she whispered. "He's behind the third tree from the second big rock. Get the scope on him."

Crap. "Uhh, I, uh, left it in the shed."

She turned and looked at me, and I swear in the pitch black of the night, I saw fire in her eyes. "What?"

"I thought you were hit."

"So you dropped your weapon?"

"I, uhmm..."

"Great, he's got us pinned down now. Unless he's a bigger Patrick than you, we're both dead."

"Give me your binoculars, I'll take care of him." Debbie handed them to me. I panned the area and found him partially hidden behind the tree. "I'll go get him, you stay here."

I belly-crawled in his direction, feeling the skin on my elbows and stomach being scraped raw by the rocky landscape, and cursed my adversary under my breath. He was going to pay for this.

I stopped every few feet to give my skin a rest and confirm that my target was still hiding behind the tree. Good thing that he wasn't skinny, or I'd have a hard time confirming that he was still cowering in his hiding place. The third time I spotted him, he pushed his hand out from behind the tree and fired a shot in our general direction without aiming.

I had to stop myself from laughing out loud. I fought back the urge to make fun of him. He must be an amateur and scared out of his wits. Too bad for him. I continued closing the distance, and when I was in range, I turned on my laser pointer and sent a 9mm slug through his shoulder. He screamed and fell backward.

I wasn't sure if he dropped his gun or not, so I approached him with caution. When I could see his face, I gifted him with another slug and ended his misery.

I got up on my knees and looked around with my night vision but didn't see anyone else. Could there be just two of them? My shoulders sagged in disappointment. All this buildup, all my high hopes, and only two dead bad guys?

Well, that freaking sucked. I was about to give up on having any more fun tonight when I heard a car start up. Yes!

Running with night vision goggles is a tricky affair, and between the uneven terrain and my new rush of adrenaline, I almost fell twice before I reached the car. It was an SUV, and I saw an old man in the driver's seat. At first I thought I was hallucinating from a lack of sleep. An old man? Really?

I'm not prejudiced against old people—I hope to be one myself one day—but if there was ever a game for young people, killing was it.

I walked up to the car and knocked on the window with my pistol. He jumped so high I thought he was going to smash his head on the ceiling and have a heart attack. I pulled open the door and pointed the laser at his chest. "Kill the engine."

He did, his teeth chattering in fear. What the hell was this old white dude doing here? With these guys? "You have some explaining to do." I grabbed his elbow and pulled him out of the SUV. I must have pulled him a little too hard, because before he could get his feet out of the car, he fell over and smashed to the ground with a loud thump. I shook my head at his ineptness and put the gun against his temple. "Name?"

"Lawrence. Lawrence Kincaid."

I gave him a quick pat-down, and he was clean. "Okay, Mr. Lawrence Kincaid. How many of you are here? Where's Cosmo?"

He turned out to be a tougher cookie than he looked, and I couldn't get anything out of him.

"Grab your laptop and come with me."

I took him up to the house and informed Debbie that all was clear but no sign of Cosmo. She came up to the front porch, looked at Larry, and made a face. "Who the hell is this guy?"

"I know, right? Anyway, I'm sure he's got a good story. Let's bring him inside."

I nudged him from behind and led him over to a chair. I cable-tied his hands behind his back, knelt behind him, and put him in a rear naked choke. I held the choke until he passed out, plus another fifteen seconds. I went to my go bag, took out two tabs of ecstasy, and placed them in his mouth.

He woke up a few seconds later, groggy and shaking his head but none the worse for wear. "What happened?"

"Sit tight. I'm going to check on your friends." I looked at Debbie. "If he tries anything, shoot him."

She smirked. "Obviously. Duhhh..."

I went outside and tracked down the first guy. As expected, there was a hole in his chest that you could pass a basketball ball through blindfolded. What a nightmare. I had to rethink my rifle acquisition. The Remington 700 had seemed all romantic when I was reading the specs and reliving Debbie's escapades with it, but now that I was thinking about the mess I had to clean up, it lost some of its appeal.

Even with the night vision goggles, I couldn't see such fine detail in the dark, but I was sure that Remington Man's DNA was scattered all over the place within a fifty-foot radius. I'd have to napalm the place to get rid of it all.

I'd known the second guy was dead when I saw the impact of my lead slug rock his head to the side, so I didn't bother confirming his demise. I walked over to my truck and grabbed my disposal bag, which contained rubber gloves, hand sanitizer, paper towels, plastic painters' drop cloths, garbage bags, and of course the number one tool that no self-respecting killer would leave home without: duct tape.

I started with Remington Man, since he was the biggest mess and I liked getting the hardest part of the job out of the way first. When I was done gathering all the body parts, I carried his plastic-cocooned body over to his SUV and tossed him in the back.

The Glock guy was a quicker cleanup, and I thanked the good Lord the whole time I gathered up his mess that I hadn't used my Remington on this guy. I tossed him in the back of the SUV as well and locked it. I went back to the house, and Debbie met me at the door.

"All clean?"

"Not really, but I got the major parts in their SUV. We have to make sure we don't leave anything of ours behind. Even in daylight, it'd be impossible to clean up the mess these guys left behind. How's Mr. Kincaid?"

"Happy as a pig in shit."

"Ecstasy will do that to you. He'll spill his guts now."

"How do you know?"

"I heard it on a Joe Rogan podcast, so I know it'll work."

"Joe who?"

"Never mind, it doesn't matter. Let's go talk to Mr. Kincaid."

Happy as a pig in shit was an understatement. Mr. Kincaid couldn't wait to tell us everything. So much so that we couldn't get him to shut up. He went on and on about all the shit the CIA had done to him, how he loved his little Asian girlfriend who had broken his heart, and how Cosmo had enticed him with hundreds of thousands in cash. He even gave us seven locations where he had cash hidden.

After more than an hour, I needed a break from him talking, so I duct-taped his mouth shut. Debbie and I stepped outside for some fresh air. My adrenaline rush had dissipated, and fatigue was starting to seep into my bones. I knew this was a dangerous time, a time when mental mistakes were made.

"Wow, that's some crazy stuff. I can't believe men pay him to do that to their wives. What should we do with him?" she asked.

"What do you mean? We kill him."

"I know that, but do you think that there's a way we can free all those women who have a GPS tracking device in their implants?"

"I guess we could get a list of them and anonymously send it to the FBI. Along with his laptop."

"That'll work. Let's just finish our conversation with Larry."

We went inside, and sure enough, we got the scoop on everything. His laptop passwords, login info, foreign bank account numbers, and payment info from the psycho husbands who'd implanted these devices in their wives without their consent.

But the most exciting piece of info I got out of him was the address of his last meeting with Cosmo.

I high-fived Debbie, thanked Larry for his cooperation and re-applied a rear naked choke. He passed out, and I duct-taped a garbage bag over his head. His lucky day. A nice nonviolent and pain free death by asphyxiation. Probably too good for Mr. Kincaid, but I had bigger things to worry about. I tossed him over my shoulder, carried him to the SUV, and threw him in the back on top of the others. I covered them all with black garbage bags and closed the hatch.

I went back inside the house. Debbie had cleaned up, turned off all the lanterns except for one, and closed and locked all the shutters. "Everything is sanitized."

"Good, let's get out of here. I'll take everything in their SUV, and you follow me in my truck. If I get pulled over, you keep driving and meet me at the old mine on Adirondack Road in Tahawus. If I don't show up within thirty minutes, head home."

44

DEBBIE TURNED off the lantern with a gloved hand and closed the door behind us. I gave her a kiss and threw the go bags in the backseat of Remington Man's SUV. I started her up and almost gagged. The stench of fried food was so bad it came out through the vent ducts, and I had to drive with the windows open to clear out the toxic air.

Tahawus was a little more than an hour's drive south, and once I left the highway I didn't see another car. Pulling into the ghost town in the dark was an eerie feeling, and I felt a shiver race down my spine. An honest-to-goodness ghost town, just like you saw in the movies when you were a kid. Except this wasn't the movies.

With Debbie following me, I found the section of Adirondack Road that passed between the two lakes that had been created from digging the mine. The lake to the south had the easier access, and I pulled over next to it. All I had to do was roll away a few big rocks that acted as a barrier to keep folks from accidentally driving into the lake. That was no easy task, but my decades of weightlifting made it doable.

I pulled out my go bags and handed them to Debbie, who put them in my truck. I put the SUV in neutral and started to push it over the side. As soon as the front wheels cleared the edge of the cliff, the big vehicle came to a grinding halt. The SUV was so long that the rear length more than balanced out the part of the engine that was forward of the front wheels, so it was hung up. I put my shoulder into it but couldn't move it an inch. Holy crap, this was bad. If I didn't get this monster over the side, my flawless record of making dead bodies disappear would be over. I thought about all the DNA evidence I'd left on the bodies and scattered through the interior of the SUV, knowing that the thousand-foot-deep water would eliminate all of it in short time, if the vehicle was ever recovered.

I changed tack and tried lifting the rear bumper, figuring that if I could raise it high enough, the weight of the tipping engine would slowly make it lighter, and I'd be able to topple it over the side that way. Despite my better-than-average deadlifting skills, I was unsuccessful in raising it more than a few inches, so no toppling forward.

Debbie grew impatient. "What the hell, Patrick? Hurry up."

"I'm trying, but I can't move it."

She came running over to lend a hand, and the two of us

grunted and groaned in our deadlifting quest, but we still couldn't get the rear end high enough to topple it over the cliff.

We collapsed from exhaustion, and Debbie said what I didn't want to hear. "You know what this means, right? You'll have to push it with your truck."

I didn't answer, but I knew it was coming to that. The only problem was that I'd need the delicacy of a surgeon to push the SUV with my truck and not go over the side myself. I had a vision of my truck following suit, me tumbling down inside of it, Debbie yelling from above, "Nice move, Patrick. I'll let Frankie know!"

"All right, but let's get everything out first. Just in case. I don't know how close I'll have to get to the edge to push the SUV over, or how much momentum I'll need to have. With this gravel surface, traction—and more importantly, braking—will be poor. I'll have to gun it and then brake hard once the SUV topples forward. Then it becomes a question of whether or not I can stop on the slippery gravel before my front wheels go over the edge."

"Better be careful of hooking your bumper over the SUV's, too. If you manage that, the rear of the SUV might lock into your bumper when it rises up and take your truck with it."

Great. One more thing to worry about. Now I'd be tumbling down, connected to my SUV buddies, and forever entombed right next to them. Talk about karma...

Enough with the thinking. I went to my pickup and

removed all of my tools, including the lead-shielded bag with the phones inside, stuck them in our go bags and laid them to the side. I climbed in and took a deep breath. I decided to leave my door open, just in case I had to get out fast.

I put the truck in four-wheel drive for better traction and inched my way forward until I felt the solid clunk of my fender on the back of the SUV. I pressed on the gas, soft at first, and my Toyota engine revved, but we didn't move. I felt the torque of the revving engine tilt my truck, but still no movement forward. I pressed the gas pedal down some more, and the engine roared louder. Nothing. I felt my tires lose their grip and they started churning in the gravel. Still no movement. Shit. I backed off the gas.

"You might have to ram her, Jack. Please be careful."

I didn't see any other way. I couldn't just leave these guys here. No matter what, I had to get that SUV over the cliff.

I backed up about thirty feet, gave Debbie a smile and a nod, and gunned the engine.

I was only going about twenty miles an hour when I struck the rear of the SUV, but the impact was terrifying. First my headlights crushed out and in the dark I had no idea how close I was to the edge. The airbags went off at the same time, and I jammed on the brakes so hard that I almost hurt myself.

I'd always been a big believer in positive thinking, complete with self-talk, as a way to tilt the odds in your favor when trying to achieve a goal or get out of a bind. All the while I kept repeating to myself, "I will stop my truck before the edge, I will stop my truck before the edge..."

Except I didn't.

At first I thought I had it made. The split second of stoppage when my truck slammed into the back of the vehicle raised my hope of a successful outcome, but, positive self-talk or not, it wasn't to be. The impact was enough to grind the SUV loose and send her flipping over the edge. It all happened in slow motion. The big ass of the vehicle raising up, teetering for a second, and passing the tipping point before flipping over and tumbling away. It was a beautiful sight, but there was little time for enjoyment.

I knew that my front tires were close to the edge, but they were still on solid ground. Yes! I put the truck in reverse, floored it, and felt the front of my pickup fall and hit the ground.

The edge of the cliff, weakened by the grinding of the big SUV, had given way.

Oh shit.

I gunned it some more, but the Toyota just didn't have the power to back its front wheels up and over the cliffside.

I pushed aside the deflated airbag, yanked my keys from the ignition, and got out of my truck. I backpedaled far enough away from the edge of the cliff to feel safe and took a knee to catch my breath and let the adrenaline stop running amok through my bloodstream. My whole body was shaking, and my hands trembled as I placed them on the ground for balance.

"Holy shit, Jack. I thought you were a goner." Debbie hugged me so tight that I fell sideways. We lay there for a few seconds, and the reality of the situation sunk in.

She placed both hands on my face and kissed me softly on the lips. She whispered, "You know what we have to do, right?"

"Yeah. I know."

I'd had that truck for a long time. Cheryl and I had bought it together after we'd started dating. I could never bring myself to part with it, but the realization that life kept moving forward and would never stop tossing remnants of my time with Cheryl overboard had never been more apparent than it was now. Each day that passed left me with fewer and fewer things in my life that linked us together, and now my truck was one of them.

I stood up and smiled at her. "I'm glad you're here with me."

Together we lifted the rear of the truck and sent her flipping over the side. A few seconds after she disappeared into the black night, I heard the loud smack of the two-ton machine belly-flopping into the water. It wouldn't take long for it to sink to the bottom and be gone forever. I made a mental note to fill out a stolen vehicle report when I got back to the office, just to cover my tracks.

We rolled the rocks back into place. I wiped my hands together a few times to clean the dirt off and smiled at Debbie. "Let's walk until we hit a cell tower."

"Who you gonna call?"

"Why, Frankie, of course."

She reached up and smacked me in the back of my head. A playful gesture that made me laugh. She followed it up with a hug. "Why not Uber? Huh?"

We laughed, partly because it was funny, and partly because the toughest part of the mission was over and we were a little giddy from being overtired. She intertwined her arm in mine, and together we picked up our go bags and started walking.

45

FRANKIE PICKED us up in my X5M with Catherine sitting shotgun. Debbie and I hopped in the backseat, threw our go bags into the cargo area, and after a few pleasantries, we dozed off.

By the time we got back to Eminence, it was late morning and Debbie had to work in the evening. She called me into our bedroom, and despite my fatigue level being off the charts, I got excited because I knew that Debbie had to shower for work, so I figured it was an invite.

She had other ideas. "Frankie was parked in my spot. That bitch."

"Honey, you need to get past this. It's not like she did it on purpose. Give her a chance, she likes you."

"Really? Oh, that's right, she'd do me. How could I forget?"

"Frankie has what you might call an overactive libido.

And just because she'd do you, that doesn't mean she likes you. But I can tell, she *does* like you."

"So how many women did the two of you sleep with?"

"Oh, come on, that doesn't matter. That was years ago, before I even met you."

"More than a few?"

I didn't answer.

"I knew it..."

"Knew what?"

She ignored my question and trudged into the shower, slamming the door so hard that the walls shook. *Sheesh...*

I knew that Frankie had to leave, so I went out to the living room. She and Catherine were sitting on the couch, the dogs by their feet. When she saw me, she hugged Catherine goodbye, and I walked her out through the garage.

"So, Jack, other than losing your ride, mission accomplished?"

"Yeah, it went well." I looked at her and smiled.

"I knew it would. Man, you look tired."

"I'm wiped out. I'm not used to going days without sleep anymore."

"This is a young man's game, Jack. You oughta think about chilling for a while. You got it good here. Your Debbie's a hot little number, and you know so many guns for hire that can take care of things for you."

"Yeah, I know, but after Flight 2262... ah, you know my deal." I looked away and thought about my murdered wife,

Cheryl. Killed in horrible fashion in an event that had put me over the edge of reason and turned me into the blood-seeking vigilante that I am today.

Frankie tugged my arm. "Jack, you can't go around killing bad people forever. You've had a great run, a perfect record, but sooner or later the odds are going to catch up with you. You're going to make a mistake that's going to come back and haunt you, or worse, a loved one."

I bristled at the thought. I didn't think I'd be able to live with myself if I didn't act on the knowledge that was at my fingertips. I sighed. "I still have more I need to accomplish."

"Suit yourself. Call me if you need anything. Oh, and Catherine's cool. She's been through a lot, but I think she'll be fine. She just needs to spend some time in recovery and with some good people instead of the dirtbags she's been hanging with."

I opened her car door for her, and she tossed her backpack in the passenger seat. She gave me a hug. "Be well, Jack."

"I will. You too."

She sat in the driver's seat, closed the door, and pressed the push-button start. The throaty rumble of a powerful engine as it came to life never got old to me. It didn't matter if it was an automobile or an airplane, it always raised my testosterone levels, and for a few seconds I forgot how bone-deep tired I was.

She rolled down her window as she drove away. "See you around, Jack Lamburt." And with a wink and a smile she was gone. I stood in the driveway and watched her tail-lights fade away, wondering if I would ever get the chance to repay her.

"Need a tissue?" I turned around, and Debbie was standing in the doorway, her hands on her hips and her head cocked to one side. Her hair was still wet, and she wore one of my XXL T-shirts, a habit of hers that I loved, especially since she'd never bothered to put on a bra under it, and it was so big and loose on her that if she leaned two degrees forward I saw what drunken Bobby could only dream about. "I hate to interrupt your Kodak moment, but I wanted to thank Frankie for all the help she's given us, especially for looking after Catherine. They hit it off well."

"Good, I'm glad. Catherine needs a friend."

Debbie came outside and hugged me from behind, wrapping her arms around my waist and kissing me on the neck. "I know I gave you a hard time about her, but she did us a real solid. Thank you, Jack."

I turned around and kissed her on the lips. One of my hands slid up inside of her shirt, and cupped her breast.

"Hey you two, get a room." Catherine stood leaning against the doorway, her arms folded across her chest, shaking her head. Buddy bolted outside with a tug toy and wrestled his way between our legs, looking up at me, and switching to Debbie when I didn't take him up on his offer. Right. Like I was *ever* going to let go of Debbie's naked breast and exchange it for a slobbery dog toy.

Debbie pushed me away and reached down, grabbing a

handful of rubber. "Come on, little gray boy, let's see what you got."

I looked down her shirt and smiled.

I went inside, unpacked, and showered. My level of fatigue had reached the point of mandatory inaction, so I lay down in my bed. Debbie joined me, and as soon as she settled in next to me, I fell asleep.

Three hours later, the alarm went off and I woke up refreshed. I lay there for few minutes and thought about what Frankie had said. About her prediction that sooner or later, my Batman fantasy life would catch up to me and come crashing down. Would I ever be able to put Flight 2262 and Cheryl's memory behind me and live a normal life? I had things most men would give their left nut for. I was a father. I had a great girlfriend and, thanks to my dad and his fast-food empire, more money than I would ever need. I was healthy—well, physically anyway—yet I couldn't quench that burning desire to rid the planet of bad people. People who inflicted unimaginable pain on the weak. On the innocent.

I felt my heart rate pick up and my pulse pound in my ears. I flashed back to Cheryl's mother, her face racked with pain, sobbing uncontrollably at Cheryl's second memorial service, the one that I was able to attend after my rescue. The roller-coaster ride of emotion that she'd endured. The happiness of her pregnant daughter's marriage and all the promise it had held in the form of grandkids. The horrific news that Flight 2262 had disappeared in the middle of the largest ocean on the planet. The euphoria of learning that there were hundreds of survivors, and the gut-wrenching pain, again, of losing a daughter.

No. There was no way I was giving up killing bad people.

46

DEBBIE and I made an early dinner and left a dish for Catherine in the fridge. She was napping on the couch when we left to head over to the Red Barn, where Debbie was bartending tonight. Saber and Buddy seemed to have felt Catherine's need for companionship, as they rarely left her side. Buddy was a little less diligent then Saber, often getting caught up in puppy play before retreating back to Catherine, dropping his favorite toy of the moment, and plopping down next to her.

I dropped Debbie off in the parking lot of the Red Barn and ran a quick errand in Richmondville. When I returned, she was already behind the bar and, as expected, working her happy hour audience. Most of the stools at the bar were taken, and another five or seven tables held food and drink for the relaxed crowd.

My Debbie was masterful at working the crowd and

building her tip jar. She was always quick to smile at their silly jokes that she'd heard many times. She held constant eye contact with those almond-shaped green eyes that left more than one tipsy fan with a gigantic crush on her and lighter in the pocket than he should have been.

My favorite was loose blouse night, where she would bend over and retrieve a frosted mug from one of the freezers that sat under the bar. Everyone within ten barstools would stop what they were doing and ogle her cleavage. I'd actually, honest to God, witnessed eyes widening and mouths opening when she did that. If she was feeling especially frisky, she'd pretend that she couldn't locate a mug and hunt around for a few seconds before straightening up. More than one patron would fidget in their stools when she did that.

My second favorite was tight T-shirt night. She'd turn sideways, raise her arms over her head, and fix her ponytail. If she was feeling particularly evil, she'd take her time and close her eyes so the guys at the bar could stare at her without the fear of being caught. More than a few of them could be seen elbowing their neighbors to draw their attention to Debbie's profile.

Tonight was tight T-shirt night, but there was no posing, or even lighthearted banter, from Debbie. Something was wrong. When she had a second to talk, she came over to me and told me what. "I messed up, big-time."

"What? How?"

"Remember the tracking device implanted in Catherine?"

"Of course." It took me a second, then it hit me. "Oh crap, where is it?"

"When we left the house in Peru with the bodies in the SUV, we were in such a rush that I forgot to take it out of my bag. I found it in there about ten minutes ago. I smashed it right away, but who knows if the signal was transmitted from Eminence? Or here?"

"Oh shit!"

47

Cosmo threw the burner cell phone across the room and cursed at it. "All my fucking guys are MIA." He turned to Amare. "Get the big boy crew together and have the Yukon gassed up and ready to roll. We're going on a road trip. If you want something done right, ya gotta do it yourself."

Amare got up from the couch and made a few phone calls, typed out a few text messages, and reported back. "All set, boss, should be good to go in thirty."

Cosmo studied his laptop, and a broad grin covered his wide face. "Well, I'll be damned. Looks like old LoJack Larry uploaded the new software." He turned the laptop so Amare could see the map, with its little flashing icons indicating the positions of all his women who had tracking devises implanted. "That one there"—he held a fat pinky on a blinking dollar sign—"that one's Catherine. Pack our bags, and let's go get this bitch."

"Bags," in Cosmo's parlance, meant weapons. Amare went into the next room and opened a closet that in a normal home would be used for hanging up the coats of visiting friends and storing umbrellas and extra rain gear. This closet was filled with weapons. He took out the Mossberg shotgun, checked to make sure that it was loaded, and laid it on the table. He grabbed a duffle bag from the floor of the closest and unzipped it. It was filled with a smorgasbord of handguns of all types. Sig Sauers, Glocks, Rugers, Colts—just about every big manufacturer had representation in Cosmo's arsenal. They all had two things in common: all were .45-calibers, and none had serial numbers.

Amare counted out enough ammo for a small war and loaded everything into a separate duffel bag, which he placed on the floor by the front door. He nodded to Cosmo. "Good to go, boss man."

They went outside, where Cosmo's men were waiting for him. He nodded gruffly to them, and they piled into the big SUV. Amare drove and Cosmo sat in the front passenger seat, using his open laptop for directions. "We're heading north. New Jersey Turnpike. Garden State Parkway. New York Thruway."

"Got it." Amare threw the vehicle into drive and pulled away from the curb.

Four hours later, they arrived in Summit. Cosmo had Amare drive up and down Route 10 a few times, past the Red Barn, to get a better feel of the layout of the small town.

"Pretty quiet up here in redneck land. This place is a freaking dive."

"I know, right? This place gives me the creeps. Let's make this shit quick so we can get the hell out of Hicksville." Cosmo pointed to Charlotte Valley Road. "Park on that street next to the parking lot and kill the engine. Stay away from that streetlight."

Amare turned off Route 10 and pulled over to the side. Cosmo turned around to face the men. All five of them, scrunched in like oversized sardines, sat with their sunglassed heads brushing against the roof of the big SUV.

"Here's the deal. Colin and Tremont, you keep watch outside in the parking lot. If anyone comes, tell them the Red Barn is closed. If they give you any shit, shoot their asses and toss them in the shrubs behind the place. The rest of you guys, come with me. Once inside, Samir, you lock the door and stand guard. Nobody leaves or comes in. Jayden, you turn off all the neon beer signs in the windows. Everyone else, follow my lead. You all square?"

They nodded and grunted their understanding, and the big Yukon creaked and elevated six inches when they climbed out. They walked around to the back of the vehicle and lined up single file. Amare handed out the weapons.

They walked along the back tree line of the almost-empty gravel parking lot. Colin and Tremont hung in the shadows, and the other five continued to the main entrance to the Red Barn. Amare reached out and pulled open the door. Cosmo stepped inside, his sawed-off shotgun leading the way, and the others followed close behind.

48

CATHERINE DIALED Debbie's number for the third time in ten minutes. Her call went to voicemail. Again. After four unreturned texts and three calls going to voicemail, she decided to call information and get the phone number of the Red Barn. She dialed that number, and it just rang and rang. She sat down on the couch, her mind racing. During this whole ordeal, Debbie had never been more than a text or phone call away. The fact that she couldn't reach her forced Catherine's imagination to run wild down a dark path. What if Cosmo had come to the Red Barn? She knew enough about him and his street cred fanaticism to know that it would get ugly fast. The full implications of the tracking device that Cosmo had implanted inside of her had hit home when Debbie explained what had happened in Peru. She'd known all along that Cosmo was a bad man, but he'd been there for her when she'd needed him most, and he really wasn't bad to *her.* She'd caught drips and drabs of his business dealings when she'd walked into rooms unannounced, causing conversations to awkwardly stop, but she wrote them off to the cost of doing business in a tough environment like Camden.

She thought of Frankie, smiled, and sent a short text to her. Deciding that a walk would be good for her nerves, she grabbed Saber's leash, clipped it on the muscular dog, and exited the safety of Jack's log cabin.

THE YOUNG MARINE, dressed in fatigue shorts and combat boots, ran up the last hill of East Road toward Eminence. He was nearing the little hamlet, his turnaround point, when he noticed a woman walking with a dog along the side of the gravel road. The half dozen or so homes he'd encountered on his run from West Kill Road to Eminence were mostly vacation homes. City folk, most from New York, coming here on summer weekends to escape the heat and nonstop rat race of the urban jungle.

This woman didn't look like your average summer vacationer. Dressed in a loose T-shirt and jeans that were a size too big for her frailness, he sensed something through her body language that raised his alert level. Something was off. If he had to guess, he'd venture that she was anxious about something.

The dog on the end of the short black leash was a Doberman pinscher, who spotted the Marine over his shoulder just as he trotted around a bend in the road. The Doberman stopped and turned around to face the Marine. The woman, off in another world, didn't hear him approaching, so he slowed to a walk when he got close to her. After a few seconds of diligent observation from the Doberman, the woman tugged on his leash. "Come on, Saber."

He didn't move, and she turned around and jumped when she saw the Marine.

"Good evening, ma'am. My apologies if I startled you," the Marine offered.

"Oh, it's okay. I'm not used to the peacefulness of the country yet. I didn't expect to see another person."

"Where are you from?"

"New Jersey."

The Marine nodded to the Doberman. "That's Saber, Sheriff Lamburt's dog, correct?"

"Yes. You know him?"

"He's a great dog."

"I meant Jack."

"Oh, yeah. I haven't seen him in a while, but Sheriff Lamburt and I go back a long way. How is he?"

"Well..." She looked down, and the Marine knew something was wrong. "He's okay, but I haven't been able to reach him."

"You try the Red Barn? He used to date one of the bartenders."

"Yes. My sister."

"Debbie's your sister? Wow, small world."

She frowned. "They left a while ago, and I haven't been able to reach them. I got into a little trouble, and they helped me out. Now I'm worried about their safety."

The Marine studied her and saw the deep concern etched in her face. "Come on. Let's go back to Jack's house. You can explain everything to me on the way."

He led the way and she talked nonstop, explaining the whole situation to him. When they arrived at Jack's drive-way, they saw the blue BMW parked in Debbie's spot. "Whose car is that?"

"Oh, that's Frankie's, an old friend of Jack's. She's the one who drove me home from the hospital and stayed with me until they got back."

When they got up to the front porch, the front door swung open. Buddy came roaring out, toy in mouth, and ran circles around first Saber and Catherine, then the Marine. Frankie stood in the doorway, one hand behind her back, her serious gaze going from Catherine to the Marine. "Who's that?"

"A friend of Jack and Debbie's. I ran into him when I was walking Saber, and I explained everything to him. He wants to help."

Frankie studied the young Marine, a look of skepticism on her face. "Why do you want to help?"

"I owe Jack Lamburt big-time, ma'am. My name's Harold. Harold Morris."

"What's your ex-girlfriend's name?"

"You mean Mary Sue?"

"So you're Harold." She smiled knowingly at him. "You're right, Harold Morris, you do owe him big-time." She pulled the Sig Sauer from behind her back and stuck it in her belt, stepping to the side to let them in. "Come inside, we've got work to do."

49

I SAW him burst through the door out of the corner of my eye, and I knew right away what was happening. Cosmo. He was tall and thick, half-muscle, half-fat. He waved a sawed-off shotgun in the air.

BOOM! He fired a blast into the ceiling, and everybody in the place jumped. One of Cosmo's men went over and unplugged the jukebox, and it was quiet for a split second before the shock wore off and the screaming started.

"Everyone on the ground, now!"

We all lay down where we were, forced to look up at the dominant positions of our captors. One of the men locked the door and stood guard next to it, waving his semiautomatic pistol at us. Another went over and yanked too hard on the neon sign strings, shutting them off and tearing the strings in the process. The others found corners to watch us from.

There were five of them, all dressed identically in dark clothes and sunglasses. Most had beards and short or no hair. They were all armed.

I calculated my chances if I drew my Glock 17 and opened fire, but the numbers were just a little too much. In the movies, yeah, no sweat. If Jack Reacher were here, all five would already be dead, stacked neatly in the corner while the beautiful big-titted barmaids took turns flashing the male patrons while they topped off their ice-cold frosted mugs with imported beer in between back rubs and hand jobs. Drinks would be on the house, and everyone, even the old white folks, would be good dancers. Burgers cooked perfectly with just the right amount of ketchup and salt and the perfect complement of crispy fries would be delivered at a perfect one hundred and twelve degrees to the giddy eaters.

But Reacher wasn't here, and I didn't feel like taking a chance on killing any innocents, so I sat tight. I looked around the room at the usual Red Barn customers, folks that I'd known for a while and become friendly with. Frances was there, as she was every night. She never left her barstool, and Cosmo probably thought that the little old granny hadn't heard him or wasn't worth shooting, because he ignored her and her lack of hostage listening etiquette.

Drunken Bobby, who still believed that he had a chance with my Debbie, lay on the floor with an Old Milwaukee in his hand. Mary Sue, college student and part-time waitress, put her tray down on a table and sat on the floor Indian-style. She looked at me, and I nodded to her. Max and Gus, the two happy old men with the sparkling eyes of youth, who, according to Frances, were great lovers, were kneeling down and pocketing pool balls. Rodney, the third-shift correction officer at the Summit Shock Camp who stopped in a few times a week *before* he went to work, sat on the floor and shook his head and cursed at them under his breath. Boy, did he pick a bad day to visit us.

They were all folks I was responsible for protecting. And I had gotten them involved in this instead. Maybe Frankie and her prediction of messing up had come true. I had no plans of giving up on my life's mission, but if I was responsible for an innocent person getting hurt, a person whose only crime was knowing me, then it was time that I packed up and left this town.

Cosmo didn't waste any time on pleasantries. He belted out, in a loud, deep voice that would have made James Earl Jones envious, "Which one of you motherfuckers has Catherine?"

50

FRANKIE TURNED onto Route 10 and drove by the Red Barn on the light side of the thirty-five-mile-per-hour speed limit. All of the neon beer signs were out. She noticed two big shadowy figures lurking near the far side of the parking lot, and when she looked inside, she caught sight of another big figure, dressed in black and wearing shades, with his back by the entrance. She nodded acknowledgment to Catherine's concern. "Yep, they're here."

A half mile down the road, she pulled a U-turn and headed back toward the Red Barn. Before she reached it, she pulled over to the side of the road, and she and Harold got out. Catherine slid into the driver's seat, and Frankie gave her last-minute words of encouragement to their visibly shaking decoy. "Just do exactly as we planned, and everything will work out. Don't think about the outcome, just focus on the process."

"Right," Catherine said. "Focus on the process."

"Give us thirty seconds, then go." Frankie and Harold disappeared into the woods.

Half a minute later, Catherine put the car in drive, pulled out onto Route 10, and headed towards the parking lot of the Red Barn.

She parked at the far end of the lot, near the lone street-lamp, with the driver's-side door facing the Red Barn. She swung open her door and threw her legs out. She wore a short skirt, high heels, and a loose-fitting white blouse that would help hide her recent breast reduction operation, all borrowed from Debbie's closet.

She played with her smartphone while the shadowy figures in the parking lot eyed her. She continued pretend-texting until one of the men walked over to her. The bigger of the two stayed behind at his post, not out of discipline, but out of laziness.

"Catherine? Is that you?"

Catherine looked up from her phone and smiled. "Oh, hi, Colin. Hey, what are you doing here?"

"What do you mean, what am I doing here? We came here to find you."

"Find me? What are you talking about?"

Colin reached down and grabbed her by the elbow. "Come with me, crazy bitch." He walked her to the front door and gestured to Tremont. "Look what I found. You stay here while I take her inside. I'll be right out."

Tremont nodded his understanding.

Frankie withdrew one of her Boker throwing knives, and as soon as the entrance door closed behind Colin, she flung it with the accuracy achieved by thousands of practice throws, sinking the knife handle-deep into the left side of Tremont's back. He reacted as if he'd been tased, his entire body tightening into one rigid piece.

Frankie was on him in a second. She jumped on his back, landing just to the right of the knife. She wrapped one arm around his meaty neck and clamped her free hand over his mouth.

He collapsed to his knees and fell forward, and Frankie dismounted before he hit the ground. She and Harold grabbed him by his feet and dragged him over behind the shrubs. She yanked the knife out of his back and rolled him over. He was still alive, eyes wide open and mouth moving like an out-of-water fish. Harold pointed his pistol at his head and Frankie held her hand out for him to stop. She knelt down and felt for the center of Tremont's rib cage. Finding the bottom rib, she placed the knife just below it and shoved it all the way in and up. She flicked it left, right, and sliced his heart into pieces.

He died with his eyes open. She withdrew the knife, slowly wiping the blood off on his black T-shirt and looking over her shoulder as she did.

"Wow, that was impressive," Harold offered. "You're pretty good with a knife."

"You should see me with an axe." She smiled and winked at him.

They heard the door squeak open and turned their attention to the entrance of the Red Barn. Colin strutted out, all smiles, no doubt having just received an atta-fuckin'-boy from Cosmo and feeling real good about himself. His smile disappeared when he looked around for Tremont and didn't see him.

"Tree?" he called out. He took the pistol out of his belt and walked over to where he had last seen his buddy. "Tree? Where you at?"

At most there was two inches between his chin and the top of his sternum. He widened the target area a little when he turned his head to the left. Not that she needed it. In one fluid motion, Frankie stepped out from behind the shrub and fired another strike, dead center into Colin's Adam's apple. He stood there for a split second, a look of wrinkled confusion on his forehead, and then pitched straight forward into the parking lot, driving the knife so far into his throat that the blade stuck out the back of his neck two inches.

Harold looked down at him and grimaced. "Damn, that's gonna be a bitch to get out."

51

I saw Catherine approach the front door, wearing Debbie's clothes, and wondered what the hell she was doing. One of Cosmos's bozos had her by the elbow. He swung open the door and pushed her inside. "Hey, Cosmo, look what I found."

Cosmo turned and lowered his sunglasses. "Catherine?"

Bozo gave her a little help from behind in the form of a smack in the rear. She lurched forward and stumbled over to Cosmo, who smiled and looked at Bozo.

"Good job, Colin. Go back outside."

Colin grinned at his boss's adulation and left. Cosmo turned his attention back to Catherine. "What happened, girl? Who took you from my house? I know you didn't run out on me."

"Oh, no. Of course not, Cosmo. I would never leave you." She smiled, hugged him around the neck, and kissed him on the lips. She turned to Debbie, her smile replaced by an angry scowl, and pointed at her. "She did it." She grabbed Cosmo's shotgun and tried to point it at Debbie, but he didn't let her. Instead he grabbed her by the waist with his free arm from behind and chuckled at her outburst.

"Easy there, I'll handle this." He gestured to one of his bozo men, who came over and grabbed Catherine by the shoulder, hauling her kicking and screaming out the door. "She killed everyone. You fuckin' bitch! I'll kill you, you fuckin' bitch!"

What the hell was she doing?

I caught on when I saw a shadow move in the parking lot, just after the door closed, and the bozo fell forward like a rotten oak. Who was in the parking lot and had just taken out Bozo? My heart sped up in excitement. Frankie?

That meant that there were only four men left.

My short-lived excitement was beaten down when I caught sight of Cosmo walking behind the bar. He grabbed Debbie by the ponytail and placed the business end of the sawed-off shotgun against the underside of her chin...

52

RODNEY WAS the first to speak up, the two-beer superman effect having lifted him from the floor and into a standing position.

"She don't know nothing. Now you leave us be. Take your kind and get out of here."

"My kind?" Cosmo's voice crackled, his eyes widened, and I could tell that he was about ready to blow a fuse. "My freakin' kind?" He removed the shotgun from Debbie's mouth and leveled it at Rodney.

Uh-oh...

It dawned on me that poor Rodney hadn't learned how to be politically correct in his choice of words, and it was going to come back and bite him in the ass. Everyone else wormed away from Rodney, but good old Rodney stood there and looked Cosmos dead in the eye.

"You heard me. Leave. Now."

Cosmo pulled the trigger, and the shotgun blasted a slug into Rodney's chest, sending him cartwheeling across the room. He slammed into the restroom door and disappeared inside.

Screams broke out, and I saw the other bozos pointing their pistols around the room, just waiting for Cosmo's order to open fire.

Cosmo pumped the shotgun and pushed the hot end back in Debbie's mouth. I cringed at the thought of how much it must have burnt her lips and the inside of her mouth.

Cosmo appeared to have lost his patience. He screamed, "Enough fuckin' around. Who hired you?" He grabbed Debbie and turned around so that her back was to us. "Three seconds and I blow her brains all over you fuckin' hick bastards," he shouted. "Three, two..."

I knew enough about Cosmo from my HFS research on him to be sure that no matter what I told him, we were all dead. But ya gotta go out swinging.

I stood up and stepped forward.

"Me. It was me. I was hired by Catherine's family in LA to get her back. I killed your men."

Cosmo turned toward me, and even in the dim lighting I could see the fire in his black eyes. He took the shotgun out of Debbie's mouth, pointed it at me, and the lights went out.

The timing was perfect. The only light coming in was from the streetlight, and I dove to my right while drawing my Glock. I saw silhouettes of the two guys standing by the door, and Cosmo with Debbie behind the bar. They didn't realize that making everyone lie down would make their silhouettes easy targets. I fired four times at the men by the door and was satisfied when I heard the solid impacts of bullets hitting bone. They both fell to the ground, one of them screaming in agony.

I turned and fired twice into the corner, where the other man was last standing. There was no silhouette there, but it was pitch black in the corner, so I didn't expect to see one. My first bullet hit him somewhere, but I couldn't tell where from the sound, and the second might have missed. I heard him collapse to the ground, so I turned to look for Cosmo.

He was gone. So was Debbie.

I felt the unmistakable round metal end of the shotgun pressed against the side of my neck, and my heart sank. A big meaty arm wrapped around the other side and put me in a standing headlock. Cosmo whispered in my ear, "Drop it." I let the Glock slip from my fingers and closed my eyes and shook my head when I heard it hit the floor. I was in big trouble.

The lights came back on, and Frankie came running through the front door and sent two more slugs into Cosmo's fallen bozos, who were crawling on the floor and reaching for their guns. Both were head shots, and they were dead before their foreheads bounced off the hardwood floor.

In the mirror behind the bar, I saw Cosmo's reflection

standing next to mine. He was smiling. "Throw your gun down and put your hands up, or I blow his fuckin' head off."

Frankie dropped her pistol and put her hands behind her head. She looked right at Cosmo, a deadpan, almost comically bored expression on her face. Frankie and I had been through a few tense and exciting rides together, and I knew she was as deadly as they came, but this was bad even for her. I hoped she wouldn't die here because of me. Wouldn't that be ironic, after her warning and all...?

I looked for Debbie, but she was nowhere to be seen. A nightmare vision of her lying on her back behind the bar, a bullet in her head, overtook me, and I couldn't shake it free. I hadn't heard any other gunshots during the melee, so that was a good sign, but it could have been a simultaneous firing.

I felt Cosmo's stinky breath on my neck and almost gagged when I smelled the horrid combo of salami and sharp cheddar cheese. He was a wheezer too.

I caught sight of Frances disappearing behind the bar. A second later, she reappeared with the shotgun that Debbie kept stowed there. I cringed when I saw her holding the twelve-gauge on us. Even if her ninety-plus-year-old eyes could lock on to Cosmo, I estimated her chances of success, and by success I meant not hitting me, at twenty percent. And that was without the smoke from the cigarette dangling from the corner of her mouth getting in her eyes.

I saw a face peering out from the small oval window in the door that led to the kitchen, and I saw him bring a pistol up to his face and aim at Cosmo. Harold? What the hell was going on here? Crap, between him and Frances, I knew I was dead.

Cosmo walked me over to Frankie, who still had that same bored "Really? Are you kidding me?" expression on her face, like she had just been challenged to a basketball game by a ten-year-old. Her self-confidence was insane, crazy off the charts. Not a twitch, a blink, a movement by any part of her body. I almost felt sorry for Cosmo and had to refrain from telling him that he should drop his gun and beg for mercy. I felt like I was watching a movie and fought the urge to go make popcorn and plop down on the couch.

When we were about ten feet away, Cosmo stopped and looked at the two dead clowns on the floor, their brains lying all over the hardwood. The dance floor sawdust had sucked up their blood and formed gritty maroon globs. He shook his head and snarled at her. "You fuckin' bitch." He swung the shotgun toward her.

Quicker than I'd ever seen a person move, she flung her right hand forward and fastballed a knife into his chest. I grinned as her right elbow rose, ever so slightly, and I realized that her hand was sliding down the back of her neck. I knew what was coming; she was Annie Oakley with a knife. It hit him so hard that I felt the bony vibration travel up his body, through his arm, and into me.

I'd seen her in action on many occasions and knew that she never went anywhere without her throwing knives nestled snugly between her shoulder blades in a custom-made holster that fit her perfectly, providing lightning-fast access to three of the perfectly balanced razor-sharp six-inch blades. They were her safety blanket, like Linus and his blanket, or Karl Madden and his American Express card.

Harold fired a single shot from across the room, and I closed my eyes and winced. Cosmo's head whipped to the side from the impact and bashed me in the temple. I saw stars and felt warm fluid all over the side of my head. Was I shot?

Out of the corner of my eye, I saw Max and Gus help each other up. Max scowled at Cosmo. He reached into his pocket and—oh God, no—he pulled out the eight ball. He went into a full windup and let it fly. I'd experienced Max's pitching prowess and knew that he had a great arm, but blasting a pool ball through the rear window of a big-ass SUV was one thing. Nailing Cosmo in the head—albeit, it was a large one—was on a whole 'nother skill level. I closed my eyes, ducked, and said a silent prayer to the gods of good aim.

I've killed a lot of bad guys in my life, and I'm not what would be called a squeamish individual, but the sound that a Nolan Ryan'ed pool ball makes when it slams into a human skull is as sickening as it gets. I admit I smiled when I heard it, partly because I was relieved that it wasn't my head, but mostly because after the initial impact, I didn't hear the ball hit the floor.

It was stuck in Cosmo's forehead.

This was some crazy shit, and I breathed a sigh of relief that it was over and I was still alive. Cosmo's dead arm was still wrapped around my neck, and I went to duck under it when I saw Frances struggling to bring the twelve-gauge up to her shoulder, aim, and pull the trigger on the big shotgun that probably weighed more than her.

This was going to hurt.

Cosmo's lower body shot out from under him, and he went airborne for a split second before face-planting onto the hardwood floor. I heard the muffled crack of the pool ball as it slammed into the floor. He was already dead three times by that point, but just the same, the vision of that eight ball being driven further into his head had me stifling a laugh when I envisioned the coroner performing the autopsy and trying to determine the exact cause of death.

I turned around and looked at the jukebox. It was covered with pieces of Cosmo. Damn, I'd never be able to play another song again without smiling. Ah, good times...

I looked down at Cosmo's body and saw a huge gap between his legs. Frances had shot his balls off.

The blast of the shotgun sent her reeling backwards, and I cringed as she went flying into the glasses and bottled spirits that lined the mirrored back wall of the bar. I flashed back to the bar scene at Sparky's Massacre and closed my eyes so that I wouldn't witness the carnage that would rain down on poor Frances if our shelving didn't do a better job of holding up than Sparky's Tavern's had.

Frances stumbled, a burst of profanity flowing out of her

mouth like a rap singer, but the shelves held. She stood up, her cigarette still dangling from the corner of her mouth. She looked around and must have sensed that order was restored, because she laid the shotgun on the bar and took a deep drag on her Lucky Strike. She poured herself a glass of whiskey and nodded to me before raising the glass and toasting me. My ears were still ringing from all the gunshots, but I couldn't help but smile at her when I heard her yell, "Sheriff Joe, bottoms up!"

But where was my Debbie?

53

HAROLD CAME RUNNING out of the kitchen and pushed me to the side. The clown who'd been standing in the corner before the lights had gone out was getting to his knees, his hand inches from his pistol. Harold let fly a single shot just as the bozo was lifting his gun to fire at us. The bullet tore into his face, snapping his head back and slamming it against the wall. He fired off a round in his death dance, but it went harmlessly straight down into the dance floor.

I picked up my gun and ran behind the bar. Frances was helping Debbie up. She was wobbly and had a big gash under her chin that dripped blood all over the front of her shirt. She had another wound above her hairline over her forehead, and her face was covered in blood. She looked like Carrie on prom night. I sat her down on a barstool and held her so that she wouldn't fall over. Frances came over with a roll of paper towels and pressed them lightly against her wounds, but that didn't slow the blood flow. Within seconds the floor was littered with red paper towels, and Frances was elbow-deep in blood that ran down her hand, dripped off her arm and pooled on the floor.

The state troopers arrived, and once the scene was declared secure, the EMTs came sprinting in, carrying their bags of life-saving equipment. The first one to enter, a young girl in her twenties, stopped at one of Cosmo's clowns and knelt down next to him. I grabbed her by the elbow and pulled her away. "Forget them, help the bartender."

She looked over to Debbie and recognized her right away. "Debbie!"

She grabbed her bag and ran over to her.

By this time, Frankie was helping with Debbie. Since she was fading in and out of consciousness, they decided that it would be best if she sat on the floor, her back against the bar for support. On the rare occasions that Debbie opened her eyes, usually only for a split second, they were blank with no focus in them. Frankie was sitting on the floor next to her, holding Debbie's head against her shoulder and talking softly to her as she held a paper towel to her head and brushed the bloody hair from her face. I couldn't hear what she was saying, but I knew that it was something reassuring.

Francis was still swapping out paper towels against her gash under her chin, and the blood flow had slowed down to the point where I could briefly see the whiteness of her chin bone between paper towel changes before the two-inch canoe-shaped opening on her chin filled up with blood again. Nasty.

The EMTs stepped in, laid her on her back, and went to work on her. Frankie stood up and came to my side. "She's in bad shape, Jack. No pupil response. Better ride in the ambulance with her. I'll grab Catherine and follow you to the hospital."

The EMTs stabilized Debbie and fast-wheeled her out to the ambulance. I could tell by their rapid pace that they feared for her. I climbed in to keep her company on the way to the Cobleskill Hospital. A somber trip, with no talking except for the two first aiders discussing business as they worked on her nonstop. I touched her ankle and squeezed it softly. No response.

I knew that head wounds bled a lot, often times making the injury look far worse than it was, but she'd really lost a bucketful of blood. I could see her broken nose swelling up before my eyes. Her T-shirt was soaked with so much blood that when they cut it off to examine her for torso injuries, it fell to the floor with an audible splash.

We arrived at the emergency entrance, and when I stepped out of the ambulance, I was surprised to see many of the other patrons from the Red Barn trotting towards us from the parking lot. They weren't here because they needed medical attention. They were here because of Debbie. They must have caravanned behind the ambulance. That's one of the nice little surprises you got when you lived in a small town, one that often went unmentioned. Folks looked after each other. They genuinely cared.

The EMTs wheeled Debbie inside, and I stood and watched my fellow small-town folk make me proud to be part of such a tight-knit community. They gathered alongside the walkway that led to the emergency room and called out Debbie's name, followed by all kinds of get well wishes. I'm not sure if she heard them, but I hoped so.

Frances screamed for her to "hang the fuck in there." Frankie was holding a sobbing Catherine in her arms, but still managed to reach out and touch her.

Even drunken Bobby, a can of Old Milwaukee beer in his raised hand and a second unopened one in his back pocket, managed to yell over to her between chugs, "I love you, Debbie."

I wasn't sure if that made her feel better or worse, or if she even heard it, but it made me smile. I often teased her about how she flaunted her physical perfection to fatten up her tip jar, how she was like a high-class ho that managed to get money even though she kept her clothes on, which more often than not led to a stiff elbow in the ribs, but tonight's show of compassion from the Summit folk made me promise to myself that if she pulled through, I'd never look down on her tip-gathering skills again.

54

THIS WAS BECOMING A COMICAL HABIT. The two stiffs in their navy Ford Taurus pulled into my driveway, stepped out, complete with cheap suits and sunglasses, and walked up to my front door. I recognized the first agent from his last visit and decided to be nice to him. I opened the door before they stepped up on my porch and didn't even point my gun at them this time. "Morning, gentlemen. How can I help you?"

The first agent took off his sunglasses and introduced himself. "FBI. Special Agent Leo Kennedy." He flashed his ID.

I nodded and smiled. "Yes, I remember you from your last visit."

"And this is Agent Russel Blake. We'd like to have a word with you."

I nodded to the younger agent, who was slightly overweight and struck me as being hungover. "Sure, come on in."

I walked them to the kitchen table, each one keeping an eye on Saber, who was watching them from the living room. He sat there, his back to the fireplace, and didn't move a muscle. He was the staredown king, never breaking eye contact with Agent Blake, who was closest to me.

Buddy came running up and jumped on Agent Kennedy, almost knocking him over. I went through the motions of a good dog owner and chastised him, but in my mind, I fantasized about Agent Kennedy backpedaling in a panic, right out the front door, falling down the porch stairs and landing with a splat in the mud. Childish of me, I admit it.

I offered them drinks, which they declined, so we got down to business. "So what can I do for you?"

We spoke for a while, Saber's stoic gaze shifting from one man to the other as they took turns speaking. They asked me if I knew anything about the Newburgh gang violence. I answered no, that I had enough to keep me busy here and I didn't follow the news. They asked about my flying experience, and I offered them both a ride in my Cessna, but for some strange reason they declined. Sheesh. Who turns down a free ride in an airplane?

They seemed very curious about how Cosmo and his gang of dead men had wound up at the Red Barn. I told them I had no clue, but that the New York State Troopers —"Now there's a real law enforcement agency for you"—

were investigating, and I was sure that *they'd* get to the bottom of this.

We bantered back and forth, and Agent Kennedy commented that they'd received an anonymous package that contained a laptop with a bunch of passwords. The laptop was from an ex-CIA agent, now missing and presumed on the run, and contained custom-built software that was used to track the breast and butt implants of hundreds of unsuspecting women. The FBI was making arrests on an almost daily basis because of it, everyone from rich husbands to crooked doctors. I appeared shocked, in mouth-open disbelief that people could do such an awful thing, then nodded my congratulations and stood up to offer them the door.

I stood in the doorway and watched them drive away. Debbie came walking out of our bedroom, steadying herself with a hand against the wall. She still had minor bouts of dizzy spells, courtesy of her concussion from when Cosmo had knocked her out when he'd slammed the butt of his shotgun into her chin. A nice scab had formed along the entire width of her chin, about a half inch wide. It was disgusting, yet beautiful. Much prettier than a bullet hole.

She'd whacked her head on one of the bar fridges on the way down, and if that wasn't enough, she'd face-planted and broken her nose. It was the perfect trifecta of pain. I didn't know which blow was worse, having not seen any of them occur, but between the three, she'd suffered a serious concussion.

Much to my relief, she was past the danger point, but she still looked she'd been hit by a Mack truck. I couldn't help but smile, though, because I got to take a few weeks off to take care of her in my house. I'd been trying to get her to move in with me for a while now, but she'd always resisted. A few words from the doc had spelled out the conditions of her release from the hospital. "You can stay at Jack's, or you can stay here. What would you like to do?" That had changed her reluctance to cohabitate.

Between my expert culinary and nursing skills, Buddy's youthful exuberance, and Saber's unyielding loyalty, I think we might be winning her over.

EPILOGUE

RODNEY MILKED his gunshot recovery for three months before he was forced to go back to work. His Coolmax II vest had worked as advertised, and other than a deep bruise that made him wince every time he took a breath, he was fine.

Bobby still woos my Debbie every chance he gets, but deep down, I know that *he* knows he has a better chance of hitting Lotto every day for a month straight than winning over my Debbie.

Frances, Max, and Gus still go to the Red Barn every night, although they claim it's not the same now that Debbie and I haven't been there as much while Debbie recovers. Max and Gus still play pool, their single dollar's worth of quarters lasting them most of the night. Frances still wreaks a lot of havoc on unsuspecting men at the bar, and the three walk home arm in arm and do what I'm working hard to forget that she told me.

Harold went back to the Marines and was recently deployed to the Middle East as part of a forward recon/sniper team. He and Debbie had long tactical talks about sniping on numerous occasions before he shipped out, so I knew that he'd rack up a lot of kills. I was almost envious...

Agent Kennedy sent me an article that he clipped from the *New York Times*. It was an investigative journalism piece on the sickos that secretly implanted GPS tracking devices in their wives' breast and butt implants to keep tabs on them. He was credited with blowing the case wide open, and received numerous awards. Everybody from the FBI to the Girl Scouts applauded his diligence in getting to the bottom of it.

Silent But Deadly Aces went by the wayside. With no Cosmo present to keep things running with an iron fist, the remaining gang members went out on their own, each grabbing a street corner to ply their ugly trade. Every once in a while, one of them was shot with a Remington 700, but before the taillights of the medical examiner's van disappeared, a new dealer showed up and staked his claim on the corner.

Some charitable soul bought the Bailey Street heroin house and turned it into a public basketball court. After he tore the house down. After he dug up the entire backyard. After he discovered multiple suitcases full of moldy hundred-dollar bills.

Cobleskill has four banks, and you should see the faces

of the tellers when I made my weekly walk into each one with five thousand dollars in moldy and stinky hundreds and asked them to swap them out for some fresh ones. The first three or four times, it was funny. After about the thirtieth time, not so much...

Frankie kept in touch with Debbie, despite her worldly travels. Funny how the two of them formed a bit of a friendship through it all. Not enough to have her over for dinner and drinks, mind you, but hey, a guy can dream.

After Debbie recovered to the point where she was cleared by the doc to travel, we flew down to Key West for a week of debauchery on Duvall Street. Thank God Hurricane Irma left the bars intact.

Catherine stayed home to look after Buddy and Saber. We're not sure what the future holds for her, but she's doing well at taking one day at a time in recovery. She's even learned to smile at me. Once in a while. I think the stacks of clean hundred-dollar bills that I toss at her on her birthday, Christmas, Thanksgiving, when there's a full moon, etc., have helped.

FREE PREVIEW; AIRLINER DOWN - AN AVIATION THRILLER

*A flight to paradise turns into a nightmare when a one-man
sleeper cell ignites his plan for revenge. Can a hand full of
passengers come through and save the day? Or are they
doomed to be a footnote in the war on terror...*

Chapter 1

December 27, 9:43 p.m.

Two hours before the event

As the big airliner climbed past twenty-four thousand feet, the air pressure detonator worked exactly as planned. In retrospect, it was all too easy. A small metal box, about the size of a child's shoebox, held the components of the bomb: a nine-volt battery, a small brick of C-4 plastic explosive, a sealed glass capsule, and a digital timer.

The box was attached to the forward bulkhead in the unpressurized nose cone of the airliner. The reduction in air pressure as the airliner climbed in altitude caused the air inside the thimble-sized glass capsule to expand until it burst. The shattering of the capsule completed an electrical circuit and started the digital timer.

In two hours, the timer would reach zero, and the nine-volt battery would fire an electrical charge to the blasting cap in the C-4. The blasting cap would detonate the C-4, and the explosion would rip apart the big airliner, sending the three hundred plus holiday vacationers to their deaths.

AIRLINER DOWN - CHAPTER 2

Five hours before the event

Inside Terminal Six at Los Angeles International Airport, off-duty airline pilot Kevin McSorley rolled his carry-on luggage over the gray tiled floor towards the check-in station at his departure gate. Midevening on a Tuesday in the week between Christmas and New Year's was a quiet time for the airlines, and he had the terminal mostly to himself. Off-key, he sang out loud, "Deck the halls with boughs of holly," as he made his way through the terminal. He daydreamed about his upcoming flight to Hawaii and the six nights he would spend in a five-star hotel with a beautiful woman. His woman. "Tis the season to be jolly..."

His iPhone vibrated in his pocket, indicating a new text message. He retrieved it, and as if on cue to verify their strong mental connection, it was Margie.

Margie: Just got in, hotel rocks!

Kevin: cool, you naked yet?

Margie: Still in the lobby

Kevin: is that a yes or no?

Margie: Sophomoric

Kevin: just at gate now

Margie: Wow, u r early. Can't wait, eh?

Kevin: u bet, baby!

Margie: Hitting the gym and then the lounge for food

Kevin: don't pick up any strangers

Margie: Define stranger??

Kevin: sophomoric

Margie: Kisses. Hurry here!

Kevin: XOXO all over

Margie: Waiting up for u w cold beer

Kevin: nice! send photo

Margie: Of coors light?

Kevin: of u naked

Margie: No, use your imagination

Kevin: roger. gotta check in now, babe. Kisses

Margie: Luv u

Kevin: u 2 ;-)

Kevin smiled, pocketed his phone, and headed over towards the gate that had "Flight 2262 LAX–HNL: On Time" illuminated above the check-in counter. He looked around at the near-empty terminal and checked the time: 6:47 p.m. He had arrived early for his 9:15 p.m. flight and looked forward to putting on his headphones and relaxing to some classical music for the first time in a while.

Kevin recognized the slim brunette ticket agent at his gate as soon as he spotted her. Tess. Her dark skin and long, slightly wavy black hair that reached down to the middle of her back were a perfect complement to her bright smile and pretty features. Close to thirty, she still showed off the athletic remnants of being a collegiate swimmer in the form of a tight body, something every man within fifty feet took notice of.

"Hi, Tess," he said.

Tess stopped what she was doing, looked up at him, and greeted him with a smile. "Well, hello, Captain." She looked him up and down, and a look of snarkiness overtook her as she noticed his unusual attire: sneakers, jeans, and a button-down Hawaiian-style shirt along with an LA Dodgers base-ball cap. "Wow, someone's letting their hair down," she said in reference to his normally streamlined and stoic captainly appearance. "Will you be joining us to Hawaii tonight?" she asked.

"Yes, I will." Kevin smiled back at her, leaned on the counter, and handed her his buddy pass, the airline employee equivalent of a general admission ticket. Even if his flight was sold out, the buddy pass allowed him to sit on the fold-down jump seat in the cockpit. The jump seat was small, and the two-person cockpit was overly snug when a third person rode along, but it got the job done.

"Damn," Tess said. An exaggerated pout appeared on her otherwise perfect face. "Wish I was going to Hawaii. I did my friend a favor and traded flights with her." Her almond-shaped green eyes looked right at him. "Now I'm sorry I did that. Your flight crew has a three-day layover in Hawaii, and a three-day layover with you would have been fun."

Gulp. Kevin's heart skipped a beat. When she turned on the charm, she had the ability to make him feel like a nervous freshman, and despite his allegiance to Margie, his brain shut down and Margie was but a faint thought. Excitement churned in his stomach like a runaway freight train, and his mind was consumed for the moment by Tess.

"Yeah, that would have been fun." Kevin felt guilty about his enticement and tried to be nonchalant. "But don't worry, I have a feeling I'll be passing through these parts again soon."

"How long are you staying in Hawaii?"

"Seven days."

"Wow, nice." She smiled at him and leaned over the counter to get closer to him, her face just inches from his. "Hey, I'm on break in about twenty. Can I buy you a Coke before you leave on your little holiday vacay? Your flight's not leaving for a while."

"Uhm, not tonight. I, uh, have some work to do before we board," he lied, and stepped back slightly to create some distance between them. He was on the verge of caving in and needed some space. "But I'll take a rain check." He followed up his rejection with a thousand-watt smile.

She leaned in closer. Some of her hair brushed against his face and feathered his nose as he inhaled. He closed his eyes and savored the moment. He thought of Margie. Guilt came, he inhaled, and the guilt disappeared. God, she smelled so good.

"You know," she whispered in his ear, her breath warm and perfect, "we can go to the pilots' lounge. I'll show you my tattoos."

Tattoos were a common thread between them, and they discussed them often. "All of them?" he replied, his nonexistent impulse control once again rearing its ugly head and sabotaging his potential relationship with a member of the opposite sex. What was he doing?

"Every. Single. One." She punctuated each word, and Kevin felt his composure wavering.

Thinking of Margie, he sputtered, "Oh, man. I'd love to, but it's just not a good time. Sorry." And with a meek shoulder shrug, he waited and looked at her with a sheepish smile.

With a deep sigh, she looked down at the papers in front of her and finished her work. It was clear to Kevin that she wasn't used to being rejected by the opposite sex and that she didn't take it well. After a few seconds, she regained her happy demeanor and smiled at him as she handed him back his buddy pass with his seat assignment. "Have a great flight, sir."

"Thanks." He took his buddy pass, grabbed his bag, and rolled it away. He fought the urge to look at his seat assignment to see if she'd stuck him in the ass of the airliner, next to the bathroom.

After finding a seat far enough away from Tess so that he could focus on his work, he broke out his laptop. Since FAA regs mandated that airline pilots could only fly one hundred hours per month, they didn't really work that much. Most wound up flying eighty-five to ninety hours per month. That left them with plenty of free time for a pilot's two favorite pastimes—getting drunk, and chasing women. Plural.

Kevin had decided early in his career that it was in his best long-term financial interest to have just one wife rather than supporting a handful of women who would eventually collect alimony from him. So to keep himself busy, and out of trouble, he'd opened an Internet store that sold pilots' supplies: sunglasses, watches, and other miscellaneous items that pilots found appealing. That had worked out well up until a few months ago—the one wife part, anyway.

He attempted to check his sales numbers for the day, but he couldn't focus on the spreadsheet. He was distracted by the encounter with Tess, and his mind drifted to his younger days. Days of opportunity.

But not now. There was too much going on in his life, and the last thing he needed was another emotional attachment. And make no mistake about it, intimacy with Tess would create an attachment that would make his personal situation look like World War III as opposed to a minor skirmish in the field.

Just the same, if she kept it up, he didn't know how much longer he'd be able to resist her.

AIRLINER DOWN - CHAPTER 3

Two hours and forty-five minutes before the event

Kevin was so excited about his trip to Hawaii that he forgot to check and see who his pilots were. He usually reviewed the flight crew lineup a few days ahead of time, and if he liked the guys, he'd sit up front in the cockpit and ride jump seat with them instead of sitting with the flying public in coach. Although uncomfortable, the little fold-down seat behind the captain's seat was tolerable for a thin person like Kevin.

He boarded the plane and looked into the cockpit, where he saw the first officer, Tom Burns, sitting in the right seat. He was chatting with a fellow in a dark suit that was standing behind the captain's seat. He didn't recognize the visitor, but Kevin had flown with Tom many times and thought of him as a good pilot. Equally important, Tom was a good cockpit mate. Sometimes the younger guys that had just gotten promoted to the bigger airliners were a little nervous or hesitant in their actions or decision making, oftentimes deferring to the more experienced captain. Kevin tolerated that, figuring that it was all part of their learning and getting comfortable with the big aircraft, but he could never tolerate a bad cockpit mate. He had compiled a mental list, a personal "No Fly With Me" list, of guys who never shut up, ranted about politics or bad exes, or were all-around miserable beings who made five hours next to them in the cockpit intolerable. Tom wasn't on that list.

The left seat, where the captain sat, was occupied by Captain Roy Peterson, a thirty-five-year veteran of the airlines. Roy turned in his seat and, with the agility of a man half his age, extricated himself from his chair. "Excuse me, gentlemen," he said as he made his way out of the cockpit.

"Bathroom already? No more coffee for you, old man," said Tom.

"You got that right," Roy said. "The caffeine might inter-fere with my midflight nap. Can't let that happen."

Tom sighed, closed his eyes, and smacked his forehead in pretend anguish at his peer's old joke. "Need new mater-ial, Captain."

Roy stepped out of the cockpit, his always present smile lighting up his face, and recognized Kevin right away. "Hey, young man," he said. "Nice to see you." He held out his hand and Kevin took it—his shake was strong and firm, like a man twenty years younger than his real age.

"Hi, Captain," Kevin said. "We going to have a smooth flight tonight? I need to catch up on some sleep."

"What, you're flying and you haven't checked the en route weather forecast?" the captain ribbed. "Seems like they'll hire anybody to drive these aluminum tubes these days."

"Ha, no, I've been a little preoccupied," said Kevin. *Yeah, with Margie.*

Roy paused, and a seriousness crept into his look, "Can I talk with you a second?" He waved Kevin away from the other passengers and over to a quiet spot in the galley.

"Sure."

"This might not be any of my business, but I heard about you and Patty, and I just wanted to tell you that I'm sorry."

"Thanks, I appreciate that."

"Don't feel bad if you need to take some time off. Clear your head and all."

"Yeah, I was thinking about that...but you know how it is. Work is good for the soul. Keeps your mind off your troubles."

"True, just as long as your troubles don't interfere with your work. But I trust that you'll know if that happens. If you ever need anything, just let me know."

"Thanks, I will."

"So how long are you staying in Hawaii?" The smile came back and Roy put his hand on Kevin's shoulder.

"Seven days."

"Nice. Bringing in the New Year in Hawaii is a real treat. Elizabeth and I did that a few years ago. It was a great time. The Hawaiian people are just so friendly."

"Yeah, I'm really looking forward to it."

"Most of our crew will be laying over for three days at the Hilton. If you want to hang with us, we have some sightseeing planned for later in the day tomorrow, followed up with dinner and drinks at this awesome restaurant that I discovered a few months ago. You're welcome to join us."

"Thanks, Cap. I'm good, though. Just going to relax and hang poolside for a few days."

"Roger that. If you change your mind, the offer is always open."

"Okay, thanks again." Kevin shook his hand and made his way back to the seat that Tess had assigned him. At the ass end of the aircraft.

Right next to the bathroom.

He appreciated Roy's gesture and he was going to miss him when he left. He hoped he'd get one more flight tour with Roy before he retired, but he kept getting shut out on his bids. The monthly bid schedule for pilot routes favored the guys with the most seniority, and most of the pilots with higher seniority than Kevin also wanted to fly with Roy one more time before he retired. Kevin had no way of knowing it, but he would never fly with Roy again.

He sat down in his aisle seat, loosely fastened his seat belt, and thought of Margie. Seven days of uninterrupted quality time spent with his soul mate. Margie's uplifting energy was the perfect remedy to his marital woes.

His daydreaming was interrupted by his vibrating phone. He took it out and saw a text message from Margie.

Margie: Room is awesome

Kevin: not flying to HNL for the room

Margie: Me neither. Taking a bath.

Kevin: alone?

Margie: Ass

Kevin: hot crew on board this flight

Margie: Bring 1 with u

Kevin: ur a perfect girlfriend!

Margie: Make sure he's young AND fit

Kevin: uhm...meant SHE crew!!!

Margie: Oh! How silly of me. Just kidding...tee hee

Kevin: now Im bringing 2

Margie: Ha! Better take your Viagra!

Kevin: we'll c

Margie: Might have 2 nap, wake me when u come

Kevin: I will w/ XOXO all over

Margie: Sleep on the flight, NO flirting! Bring energy. NO excuses!

Kevin: kisses baby

Margie: XOXO!!

Kevin heard the solid thunk of the cabin door as it was closed and secured in place. A few minutes later, he felt the firm nudge as the tug connected with the nose gear of the big airliner and pushed it back from its gate. He heard the familiar soothing sound of the jet engines starting, and the aircraft started its taxi.

One of the ladies from the cabin crew came on the intercom and began her preflight announcements to the passengers, which included the locations of the emergency exits, the reminder that your seat cushion was a flotation device, and best of all, instructions on how a seat belt worked, just in case there was a Neanderthal on board.

Captain Roy came on the mike and, with the authority that only a seasoned airline pilot possessed, advised the flight crew to take their seats: "We're number one for takeoff."

On the runway, the two engines spooled up smoothly and the familiar feeling of being pushed back in his seat as the airliner accelerated made Kevin feel at home. The tires bumped along the runway expansion strips, getting softer and softer as the wings started to rise and take on the weight of the big airliner, and then silence as the nose rose and the massive two hundred and fifty tons of machine defied the laws of physics and took flight. The landing gear was raised, completing its journey into the wheel wells with a solid thunk, and the flaps were retracted.

The symphony of events that culminated in flight helped Kevin shake off the negativity of the past, and he plugged his headset into his iPhone and relaxed to some classical music. He closed his eyes and thought of Margie, and his mood elevated even higher. He relished the feel of her breath on his cheek, the excited way she hugged him when she saw him, the tenderness in her touch. She was perfect for him in every way.

Except that she was married...

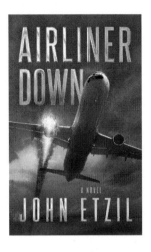

A flight to paradise turns into a nightmare when a one-man sleeper cell ignites his plan for revenge. Can a hand full of passengers come through and save the day? Or are they doomed to be a footnote in the war on terror...

AIRLINER DOWN EDITORIAL REVIEWS

"Airliner Down is a tight thriller, told with meticulous details and furious with action."

"Action-packed and full of gripping scenes and unforgettable dialogue, the book is a true feast for the mind"

"John Etzil's fast-paced and exhilarating thriller Airliner Down is not a book for those with aerophobia"
   - *Clarion Review*

"AIRLINER DOWN is a *fast-paced thriller in the spirit of Ward Larsen's PASSENGER 19. It starts strong with a gripping prologue and keeps ripping along until the last chapter.* Author John Etzil has an insider's knowledge of cockpit politics as well as airports and airplanes. So there's an authenticity going for it as well, making for a turbulent and fast read."

-Judge, 5th Annual Writer's Digest Self-Published eBook Awards

"**A gripping thriller.** With such an adrenaline-filled premise, and a shocking first chapter, **readers know they are in for a page-turning treat,** and Etzil makes good on that promise throughout."

"This thriller **feels *very* real** and more than plausible, which makes it **difficult to put down.**"

"By the end of the book, **you'll be eagerly searching for another novel from Etzil, who masterfully mixes sympathetic characters with super-charged drama to create a story that is truly memorable.**"
    - Self-Publishing Review

"Keeps you sitting on the tip of your chair!"

"The dramatic event itself and the attempts to prevent the crash gives the reader a good insight in what can happen in reality and **is told in a terrifying way.**"

"**For lovers of thrillers and aviation** it is nice reading especially when reading it in a safe place on the ground preferably not shortly before your flight departs."

- Aviation Book Reviews

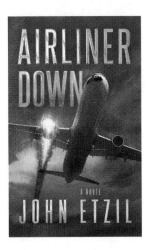

A flight to paradise turns into a nightmare when a one-man sleeper cell ignites his plan for revenge. Can a hand full of passengers come through and save the day? Or are they doomed to be a footnote in the war on terror...

FREE PREVIEW, OF A FREE BOOK; FATAL JUSTICE, CHAPTER 1

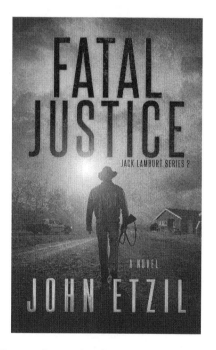

FREE - A small-town sheriff's dark secret may be the only thing that keeps his town alive...

I killed an FBI agent last week.

I had nothing personal against the agent and I wasn't proud of what I'd done, but it wasn't my fault.

It wasn't like in Hollywood, where the FBI storms into an arrest situation, everyone sporting one of those dark blue windbreakers with FBI stamped across the back in big white letters so large that a guy could read 'em from two blocks away.

Nor did the dead agent come screeching up in a cloud of tire smoke along with twenty other dark-windowed SUVs and jump out with a megaphone, announcing their arrival.

None of that really mattered though, because I was put in a position where I had no choice.

FATAL JUSTICE, CHAPTER 2

I was hanging out in my favorite bar, the Red Barn. Yeah, I know, corny name, but it *was* a red barn, built in the late 1800s and located on Route 10 at Charlotte Valley Road in the quaint little town of Summit.

Sometime around the turn of the century, the owner of the red barn had decided to throw in some light fixtures, add running water and a toilet, install an oven to warm up finger food, and build a bar close to the front door so you could grab a stool and get drunk as soon as you walked in. Not much else to do on a Friday night in upstate New York.

A three-songs-for-a-quarter jukebox sat between the sawdust-covered shuffleboard table and the lone restroom, belting out country tunes on a crackling speaker. "Elvira" and Garth Brooks having friends in low places were the two most popular. If it happened to be a holiday weekend, there was usually a live band playing, and "Elvira" and Garth

Brooks having friends in low places were the two most requested songs. What can I say? Summit had its share of simpletons.

The locals drank beer and danced to their favorite songs until they were too drunk to move. Come closing time, they'd stagger and weave their way home, most of 'em staying on their side of the faded double yellow line that ran down the center of Route 10. It wasn't pretty, but that's all we had in our quiet little town, so we were happy to have it.

"Can I freshen that up for you?" the bartender asked. She looked at me with those sultry almond-shaped eyes, courtesy of her Japanese mother, that made me melt every time she made eye contact with me. I felt knee-wobbling weak around her, but I thought I did a good job of hiding it.

"Nah, I'm good for now. Think I'll play a little pool, though. Can I get some quarters?" I whipped out a five and handed it across the bar to Debbie. She sauntered over to the cash register and I admired the snug fit of her Levi's. I didn't bother raising my eyes or killing my grin when she turned around and came back with my night's worth of pool table money. She was used to me undressing her with my eyes, so she didn't bother to comment. Her sly smirk said it all.

She placed the quarters on the bar in front of me. "Good luck at the pool table," she said. "Those guys look like players to me." She gestured over to Max and Gus, the two old men that were smacking the balls around the beer-stained pool table as if they were playing bocce ball. "I wouldn't play them for money if I were you."

They were at least two times my forty-three years, but they moved pretty well and still had a bright sparkle in their eyes. Ice-cold beer worked wonders.

"Yeah, thanks. If I lose my pickup truck to them, I'll be counting on you to give me a lift home."

"Oh, I'm taking you home anyway, unless Frances over there gets to you first." She turned to the other end of the bar and waved, her arms swinging overhead like she was waving off an errant F-18 that was attempting to land on the deck of the USS *Stennis* on a stormy night.

I looked over and there she was. My number one fan. She must have been pushing ninety-five, but goddamn, she still drank whiskey by the shot glass. She sat ramrod straight on her barstool and sucked on a Marlboro Red. At least she'd switched from those filterless Lucky Strikes.

She caught me looking over at her and winked at me, an exaggerated gesture that looked like she was having a stroke. Oh, jeez. She waved and called over to me. I cringed, praying she wouldn't lose her balance and fall off of her stool.

"Sheriff Joe, come drink with me." She raised her glass and smiled. "I'm buying."

Sheriff Joe retired a few years ago. Nice enough guy, but aside from being about a foot shorter than me, sporting a walrus mustache that complemented his combover, and carrying around a gut twice as big as mine, he looked just like me.

Ever the polite civil servant, I grinned back and raised my mug. We made eye contact through the smoky haze, and her toothless grin widened to the point of nausea. Ugh. She had probably been attractive sixty years ago, but old age and dementia didn't excite me like they used to, so I kept my distance from her.

She was nothing if she wasn't persistent. If I had a dime for every time she grabbed my ass when I made my way to the restroom, I could've retired. I swear she took the stool at the end of the bar every night so that she could reach out and touch all the men that walked by her to get to the restroom or the jukebox. Or the ones who just happened to be unlucky enough to walk past her before being warned about the Frances Fondle.

I shook my head and turned back to Debbie. She was grinning like the cat who ate the canary.

"Thanks for that. I owe you one."

"Sure. Anytime." She blew me a kiss, flashed her killer smile, and went off to pour a drink for one of her many fans who spent their nights across the bar from her, getting drunk and savoring the eye candy. Everybody loved Debbie. I couldn't blame them. What's not to like about a beautiful woman who laughed at all of your drunken one-liners?

Okay. I admit it. When we first started dating, I was a bit jealous at all the attention she received from the male patrons, but I'd grown and I was mature enough to handle it. Sometimes.

We'd been dating on and off for over a year and had talked about moving in together, but neither of us were ready for that, so we killed that idea. My hesitation was from some past relationship baggage, along with a few other issues I had. Nothing major, but they still needed to be addressed before the start of cohabitation.

I wasn't sure what her reluctance to live with me stemmed from. We enjoyed each other's company and got along great. Most of the time. We had many mutual interests. Hiking, working out, the great outdoors, dark beer, red wine, gin, whiskey, relaxing with a good book in front of a warm fire on a cold night, Barry White, love of animals, especially dogs. And hot sex. Man, did we light up the planet.

That wasn't enough for her, though. Maybe it was the age difference, me being ten years her senior? I don't know. I'm almost six foot six inches and still in great shape. Not as good as when I played basketball at Notre Dame, but still better looking naked than most men half my age. I silently toasted Arnold Schwarzenegger, whom I'd idolized growing up. He'd turned me on to weight training when I was just a kid, and man, does that pay huge dividends. I flexed my pecs and drank some beer.

Maybe Debbie was thinking longer term? As in, when she turns seventy, I'll be eighty? Perhaps, but damn if we weren't smoking hot together right now. Have I mentioned that? After a glass of red wine and a little Barry White, she looked at me with a sultriness that all my pole dancer friends combined couldn't equal.

I looked at her one last time before heading over to play some pool, and I regretted it right away. A drunk named Bobby was leaning across the bar, a dirty hand cupped tight to Debbie's ear, no doubt whispering something inappropriate. I saw her lean away and laugh right before I rolled my eyes. Jeez.

She played along like a good bartender, and guys like Bobby always left her a big tip before stumbling home, flopping into bed with their flannel shirts and jeans still on, and wet-dreaming of my Debbie.

I grabbed my beer and walked over to the pool table.

"Evening, gentlemen." I placed a dollar's worth of quarters next to the money slot.

"Howdy, Sheriff Jack. How's business?"

"Nice and slow, just the way I like it." I raised my glass and silently toasted the lack of criminal activity in our neck of the woods. Lots of folks think that being a sheriff in a peaceful no-stoplight town would be boring. They'd be right. But I've had enough excitement for two lifetimes, so I'm perfectly fine with my simple existence.

Mary Sue came over to me, put down her serving tray, and gave me a big hug. "How's my favorite sheriff?" Her mom, Meredith, and I have known each other ever since we went to Richmondville High School together more years ago than I cared to count. Spitting image of her mom, too. A little taller, about five-ten, curvy, dirty-blond hair, and a warm smile that invited everyone into her circle.

"Wow, it's great to see you." I grinned and gave her a fatherly hug. "How've you been? How's college?"

"Good. Eh, it's okay." She shrugged.

"Boys treating you well?"

"Heck yeah, once I tell them that my Uncle Joe's a sheriff." She loved digging on me about Frances's inability to remember my name.

"That's good. Tell 'em about my gun collection too." I winked at her.

"Oh, don't worry, I do."

"Mom and dad good?"

"Yeah, they're fine. They just left for their annual Florida jaunt."

"Key West?"

"Yep, fisherman's paradise. You know my dad and his fishing."

"Yeah, I do. Kindred spirits, he and I."

Stuart is a well-known cardiac surgeon and works in Albany, a fifty-mile trek up Route 88. They live in a spacious but modest two-story colonial on over sixty acres that adjoin Clapper Hollow State Forest. When he's not mending broken hearts, he's planning his next fishing trip to the Keys.

"That's true," she said. She smirked and turned a little snarky on me. "He's *almost* as bad as you and your hunting trips."

"Hey, don't be jealous now. Just 'cause I pack up my rifles every summer and fly all over the place killing ferocious animals, that doesn't make me a bad person. At least I feed the needy." I raised my mug and toasted my annual meat donations to the local food banks.

"Yeah, that's swell of you, but you disappear for like eight weeks at a time."

"So? Wait a minute... You miss me, don't you?"

"You go by yourself and nobody knows where you are. What if something happened to you out in the wild?"

"Aww. You worry about me. That's sweet, Mom."

She laughed at my teasing. "Fine. Be that way. I have to get back to work. See you in a bit." She grabbed her tray and went to take an order from a young couple two tables away. What a great kid. Her parents did a fantastic job raising her.

I sat down on a stool, my back against the wall, and watched the two ball-smacking grandfathers engage in teenage banter while they took turns missing shots. I've always loved math, and after a few minutes I calculated that they each averaged seven missed shots before they sank a ball. My quarters were going to last me a long time tonight.

In between the errant shots, I glanced over the pool table, across the sawdust-covered dance floor, and into the far corner of the room. That's the real reason I was sitting here. Playing pool was fine and all, but if I measured that up against sitting at the bar and chatting with Debbie all night, I'd pick ogling her every time. But not tonight. I needed to watch someone, and this was the perfect position to observe without being noticed.

I spied on the three middle-aged men at the corner table for a while, and as the night wore on, I felt a bad feeling grow in my gut that our long run as a sleepy little town was about to end.

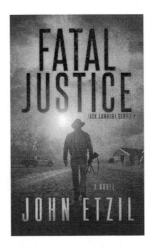

FREE - A small-town sheriff's dark secret may be the only thing that keeps his town alive...

ALSO BY JOHN ETZIL - AIRLINER DOWN

Airliner Down - An Aviation Thriller

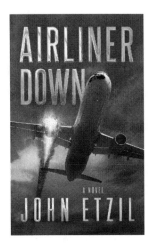

A flight to paradise turns into a nightmare when a one-man sleeper cell ignites his plan for revenge. Can a hand full of passengers come through and save the day? Or are they doomed to be a footnote in the war on terror...

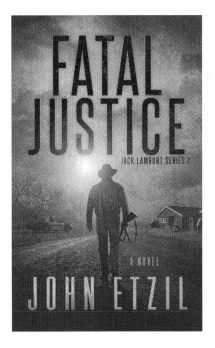

ALSO BY JOHN ETZIL - URGENT JUSTICE

URGENT Justice; Vigilante Justice Thriller Series 3.5 with Jack Lamburt

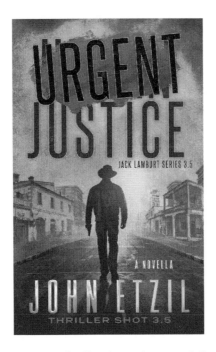

A small-town sheriff will catch a predator come hell or high water...

FREE BOOK - EXCLUSIVE TO MY READERS

Join my VIP Readers Group and get Fast Justice, a 20K word "Thriller Shot"!

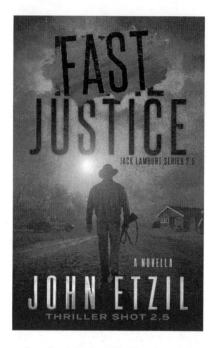

Are you up for a free John Etzil Thriller Shot? Jack Lamburt's back in "Fast Justice", and he's better then ever. Debbie steps up her game as well in this twenty thousand word fast paced thriller that is FREE to my readers. Get it NOW!

FREE - And only available to my email list! FAST Justice - Vigilante Justice Thriller Series 2.5 with Jack Lamburt!

JohnEtzil.com

ACKNOWLEDGMENTS

To my Advanced Reader Team, the best beta readers in the history of the planet earth. Thank you for taking the time to read Urban Justice and offering your input.

To Joanna Penn and the Creative Penn Podcast: Thank you for all your help in going Indie. Our whole community owes you big time.

To my readers: **THANK YOU!**

One of the rewards of being a writer is hearing from fans. If you have a minute I'd appreciate a review.

Until next time ;-)

ABOUT THE AUTHOR

John was introduced to Agatha Christie in the late seventies, and became a life long reader of mystery and thrillers after he read Murder On The Orient Express.

His favorite book is Deliverance. His favorite authors include Nelson DeMille, Russell Blake, fellow New Jerseyan AND Hungarian Janet Evanovich, Barry Eisler, Max Allan Collins, J.A. Konrath, Wayne Stinnett, Mark Dawson, Lawrence Block, and Lee Goldberg, but he'll entertain anything with airplanes, Jiu Jitsu, badass women with tattoos, big manly dogs, and tons of action!

His first novel, Airliner Down, was drafted in the summer of 2015. After numerous rewrites, he released it in March of 2017.

Fatal Justice; Vigilante Justice Thriller Series 2 with Jack Lamburt, was written during the Airliner Down rewrites and also released in March of 2017.

FAST Justice; Vigilante Justice Thriller Series 2.5 with Jack Lamburt, is a FREE 20K word "Thriller Shot"

Urban Justice; Vigilante Justice Thriller Series 3 with Jack Lamburt, was released in November of 2017.

URGENT Justice; Vigilante Justice Thriller Series 3.5 with Jack Lamburt, is a 28K word "Thriller Shot" and was released in October of 2018.

First Justice; Vigilante Justice Thriller Series 1 with Jack Lamburt, was released in December of 2019.

John is a commercial rated pilot with over twenty years of flight experience. He is an avid weight trainer and holds a purple belt in Gracie Jiu Jitsu.

He currently resides in New Jersey with his bad ass wife, two teenage sons, and two medium sized dogs.

www.JohnEtzil.com

Made in the USA
Middletown, DE
05 October 2021